Morehead
By
Jeffrey Hickey

Copyright © 2012
&
Big-n-Boo Productions

CONTENTS

1.	College	5
2.	The First Blow Out Evening	15
3.	A Laundry List of Love	30
4.	You Fool	37
5.	Last Chance for the Hippo	44
6.	Jesus and Me	54
7.	The Way Things Are	67
8.	Impulse Shopping	73
9.	So This Is Christmas	76
10.	Work in the Eighties Part 1	78
11.	Roger's Place	88
12.	Mothers	100
13.	Final Project for Speech 551	129
14.	Two Cents' Worth	155
15.	Connie and Jessica	160
16.	Work in the Eighties Part 2	163
17.	I Wish I Brought a Camera	168
18.	Thank You	183
19.	Work in the Eighties Part 3	185
20.	Don't Ever Fuck With Me, Asshole	197
21.	Way Past Life	208
22.	The Final Blow Out Evening	217
23.	Reminders	232

Preface

This story is abridged from the journals, classroom assignments, notebooks, and cassettes of Dave Morehead, a straight young man living in a gay old city.

To all the boys, whom I still see from time to time.

College

First day of the 1978 fall term in my junior year. I'm in a new school. Good God Damn Christ, here we fucking go again. It's 8:20 in the morning and the teacher might as well be talking to mannequins. The name of the class is Rhetoric and our professor is full of it. What sort of stimulant is he using to be so wired at this hour on a Monday morning? I have never in my entire life capably functioned at this hour unless utilizing a hard-on. Even years ago, when I was still routinely getting eight hours of sleep, I was barely communicative before 10:00 a.m. But this guy doesn't even have coffee on his desk. How can this be? And he wants us to care. He really does. Rhetoric is everything, he just said. He is apparently unaware of the thirty-five or so people in this classroom who don't give a shit, at least not yet.

When I was growing up, one of my wishes was for the elimination of all 8:00 a.m. classes from scholastic life. I would have lived a far saner existence. I probably would have gotten better grades and ended up at Stanford, not San Francisco State. But that's where I am, and for the last twenty minutes I've been wondering what could jar me out of my stupor and into something resembling interest.

This was easily achieved when I looked around the classroom and discovered that I am serving as fodder for at least six men glaring at me with hunger belying the hour. Of course, hunger like that knows not what time it is, only that it is time.

What did I think would happen? I'm in San Francisco, six foot two, 165 pounds, with a lithe, wiry frame utterly without fat, sporting stylishly groomed brown/blonde hair, wearing khaki shorts and a tight tee shirt that says **I ♠ My Cat** across rock hard pecks and nipples that always seem to be reaching for the coastal fog. What was I thinking when I put that on? That I'd be inconspicuous? Calm down. It's flattering. They think I look hot. Maybe I do. If they think I look hot, chances are some women will think I look hot, too. Granted, some of them will not be hot. But some of them will and, to this point, not one of them has met me. No one has formed an opinion of me. No one has branded me as anything other than how I look at this moment. I haven't opened my mouth and destroyed the illusion. And I look hot. At least, to six men I look hot. It could be six women looking at me with curiosity and hunger. Imagine that? Six women looking at me like they'd do me right now if I gave them the slightest hint of wanting, if I got up and went to the men's room and it was empty and they followed me in there and we all went into the handicapped stall . . .

Oh yeah, like that's going to happen. Ever. Like a woman would behave like a guy in these situations. Like the six, no, Christ, make that eight guys staring right now. They'd follow me in a heartbeat. They'd tear the very clothes from me, stretch my reluctant member to its maximum, then drain me dry while definitively redefining for me what it means to take it like a man, and I'd never be the same again, and I'd walk funny, and my roommate would take one look at that walk and know exactly the reason why and make me move out, and Get A Grip!

They are not going to rape me. They are not going to touch my member or me. They are not even going to hit on me because I am not going to look at them. Not ever. I can't make them stop looking at me because I'm hot and that's not a bad thing. I should be pleased. I really should. Just don't look at them.

But don't look scared, either. Because they are men and they will sense my fear and they will know and . . .

What are they going to do? They aren't going to do a goddamn thing. I'll kick their fucking hemorrhoids up to their rib cages if they so much as leer at me. I AM OFF LIMITS.

But I don't want them to hate me, either. I shouldn't look at them like I'm about to beat them and their mothers. What did Toni the hairdresser in Westwood say the last time he styled me before the move? He said that many women love gay men. They love to talk with them. They love to flirt and be friends with them, and they won't respect any man that has a problem with them being friends with gay men. He also said this was partially because many women wanted to fuck gay men, because they were so cute and mostly OFF LIMITS. (Just like I am to gay men.) He added this would especially be true in San Francisco.

Toni was a proud, flag-waving cocksucker, but I also always thought he was a very smart man, and not just because he showed me how to cover the beginnings of a bald spot without looking like some idiot doing a comb-over. In his professional opinion, this advice was going to come in handy for me someday, and sooner rather than later. But he never hit on me, not even once. Though he warned me that with hair so stylish and pecks that hard, what did he say? Oh yeah, he said the boys were going to sniff me out. He also advised me to never, ever get drunk and pass out in the house of a gay man, or else I might wake up with my dick in the mouth of someone with a mustache. We giggled like schoolgirls, but he almost snipped off part of my ear when I told him I'd already awakened with my dick in the mouth of someone with a mustache and her name was Rita.

But on the other hand, who is that redhead in the front row? Hello there. She turned around a few seconds ago and I only caught a glimpse but that was enough for me. Men? What men? Who gives a fuck about men with a redhead in the front row? Pale white skin with a sprinkling of freckles around the promise of rosy nipples and still more authentically red hair. If only she'd turn around again and look at me. What can I do to get her attention?

What are you, still in high school? Get a fucking grip and calm the hell down. It's only your first day and you're shitting yourself.

And what is this guy going on about? What is he saying? What is he on? Benzedrine? Blah, blah blah, blah blah, the world is defined by its rhetoric. Oh that's catchy. Where'd he get that? Who'd he rip that off from? He acts like he thought of it himself in order to dazzle the damsels seated beneath him, while he stands all powerful and knowing and just a salt-and-pepper goddamn aphrodisiac of credibility.

Wait a minute. Now I get it. There are four women near the front in their late thirties to early forties and they are staring the professor down. They are undressing him right now and he is letting them. You fucking silver-tinge-haired hound dog. Okay, I understand. You don't need stimulants with sex staring you in the face. He looks to be in his mid-fifties, but he's a distinguished looking fucker. Wait, check the class schedule. Yes! I'm right. He's a doctor. He's got a PhD. He's a salt-and-pepper doctor with a taste for the younger tang. And he's not wearing a ring. Oh, and look at the women. They want him. Nothing breeds moisture like perceived success and stature. I ought to listen to this guy. He's got them ever so delicately by the short hairs. And a couple of them are pretty fine—wedding rings, crow's-feet, and probably some stretch marks notwithstanding. I've had older women. They have more flaws than younger women, but they're ravenous. In my experience, they are far hungrier than younger women, who with few exceptions are either frightened or repulsed when face-to-face with a cock and balls. Maybe it's because older women are used to working with softer material from the start, and they've acquired the skills, perhaps even the taste, for reconstituting pliable meat into old-growth redwood.

All right, I really, really need to get a grip here. I probably should be listening, but I need to beat off. At least I'm taking notes. The professor and everyone else around me must think I'm just a furious, furrow-browed, note-taking stud. I hope no one can see what I'm writing. Do I dare take a glance?

WHO THE FUCK WAS THAT? Who was that walking by our open classroom door? That was one of the most beautiful women I've ever seen. And she smiled at me. She stopped, looked in the class, our eyes met and she smiled at me. Then she glanced at the information on the class posting outside the door, smiled at me again, and walked down the Humanities, Language and Literature (HLL) hallway. I've got to find her. Screw the redhead.

Well, if you insist. But seriously, that woman was stunning. Shit, I should be out tracking her down and talking with her right now.

Not so fast, Spartacus. The redhead just looked at me, and holy mother country of Ireland, she's a beauty, lads. She looks to be about five foot eight, and she's got thin ankles. That's a good sign. Skinny ankles on women equal a chance for shapely legs, that's a fact. Same thing for butts, but I don't mind a big butt if the legs still have shape. No fucking piano legs for me. When you can't tell the ankles from the calves, you don't know what direction you're heading. So ladies, if you've got big ankles, start looking for men wearing truck driver hats with a taste for American beer. Lots of it. They won't care. But I do.

Okay, so what else is going on? What class do I have next? How many more days until winter break? Why do I have to go to school?

But college is different. I know that. Since I've been in college, getting laid is always in play. I've even managed to get good grades. Granted, that was in a junior college before I came here, but I earned those grades. I did good work. I might even be developing some actual, though still mostly undefined and utterly raw skills.

And those would be . . . what exactly?

Never mind that, Dr. Salt and Pepper just spoke to me. I looked up, and at that moment he was pointing at me and telling the class they would be well advised to take notes as furiously as I am. Then he smiled at me. What kind of fucking smile was that? Was he thinking that he's glad to have me in his class? Was he thinking that he wants me in his ass?

No, no-no, no-no. I know what he's doing. He's looking for an ally. He's looking for someone he can count on from day one to toe the line and buy the whole student/teacher thing.

Or maybe he's on to the fact that I'm completely in my own world back here, could give a shit about what he's saying, and am potentially way cooler.

Only time will tell, but at this moment I know one thing for certain. I owe him.

Because when he looked at me, painted me with praise and drew the attention of every single member of this class in my direction, he allowed me the opportunity to meet and hold the eyes of the redhead, and she has to be the fairest in at least a tri-county region. She is beautiful, and she looks like she would not mind having her bonny potato field plowed. And if I'm not mistaken, it looks like she's already been plowed and that's a good thing. No more virgins please. Yes, and that dark eyeliner spoke volumes. What did my roommate call it? He said he liked his women with just a hint of sleaze. Damn, that said it all. We like them just a little sleazy and not virgins. That's because virgins are sometimes less than satisfying sexually and mostly treacherous emotionally. At least, that's been my experience.

There was one notable exception to that rule, of course. Her name was Amy and she was a virgin until the night before she left Los Angeles to start college at Harvard. She called completely out of the blue one bright and sunny August morning and without ever having met my mother before, she insisted and convinced Mom to wake me up and put me on the phone. I was supposed to work that night at a local grocery store, but after hearing what Amy wanted—including stud service and a ride to the airport—I decided it had been a long time since I'd had the 24-hour stomach flu. This was tricky. It meant calling in sick to work, but telling Mom I'd be out all night because they switched my schedule and I had to work the graveyard shift stocking shelves. Of course, I had no problem with the lies, or even possibly getting caught and losing my job, if it meant getting laid. And based on Amy's plan, it meant getting laid more than once, or at least for what she assured me would be as many hours before her parents came home from a dinner party.

She told them she had packing to do and would not be able to attend with them. She told me she did not want to go to college still a virgin and would I please do her this favor? What's a guy to do? I'm as noble as anyone and it was such a simple request. Granted, we had not gone to the same high school and only knew each other from a couple of parties in the first weeks following graduation. Luckily, we'd made out at one of the parties and groped each other a bit, but that was it. We exchanged phone numbers, but until that day neither of us had called. I wasn't sure I'd have recognized her face in a crowd. But she was offering her virginity and that was enough for me. Also, by some serendipitous miracle, I hadn't beaten off in about three days, so my love larder was full.

I lied to Mom, called in sick to work, and knocked on Amy's door precisely as directed at 8:30 that evening in my work clothes. She was wearing nothing. The plan was to have at it until we heard her parents come home, then wait for them to go to sleep before I'd leave. It was a fine plan and the evening was delightful, especially after we got the first one out of the way. There was only one problem. After several hours of vigorous aerobic and sometimes acrobatic activity, we both fell asleep and did not hear her parents come home. So when we roused from our extended catnap and started going at it again, we did not know her parents were just down the hallway. We could not tell when they turned on their bed stand light and began listening to what they assumed at first were boxes being banged against the walls. We could not hear them beginning to converse when they realized the grunts of exertion were turning into the groans of pleasure. We clearly were unaware when they rose from their bed, put on their robes, and tiptoed down the hallway as our frenzy approached another zenith. At least they had the courtesy to wait until we were completely finished and had collapsed side by side in the sweat and secretion to begin pondering how many more times we could do this before her mom and dad came home. That's when her parents walked in and turned on the light. We were both so surprised and spent that we did not bother to cover or move.

Amy said, "Mom, Dad, this is Dave. He's giving me a ride this morning."

Her mother stared at my rapidly receding member as her father calmly and sarcastically stated, "No kidding."

They retreated and closed the door, but before I could begin my sprint to dress and leave, Amy begged me to stay. She said that if I left, it would be hellish for her. But if I stayed, they would say nothing and do nothing and it would all be okay. I don't know why I believed her. It might have been the near exhaustion. So I stayed and we discreetly had a muffled one. Then we smelled food being cooked and decided to get up. It was a quiet breakfast and probably not what either Amy or her parents envisioned for her last meal before leaving home. But the only real moment of tension came when I asked her father to pass the marmalade and he glared at me while slamming it down within my reach. I said thank you then, and again to both parents when I finished. I got up, went to Amy's room, grabbed as many suitcases as possible, and waited for her by my car. About fifteen minutes later, she came bounding out of her house and sat close to me on the bench seat of my '65 Chevy Caprice. It felt like we had been going together for some time and were out for a romantic day on the coast. We laughed about her parents and only stopped once on our way to the airport. That was in the Marina Del Rey, after Amy instructed me to find someplace deserted where we could do it in the car, because she wanted to know what that was like as well.

The remainder of my virgin experiences, with one exception that I'm not going to write about now, have not quite measured up to that one. Though it must be said, that memorable August night led to my first publishing credit, albeit with a pseudonym, in the Penthouse magazine readers forum.

Okay, okay, I've got to take some precautions here. If someone in this class reads what I've been writing—someone other than a heterosexual male with a condition of semi-inflation and almost constant dripping like mine—it would be all over. In time, apologies might help, and in another year a new crop of women will arrive that do not know me, and I might be able to get to them before they hear about me and what an asshole I am. But why risk it? Turn the page and start taking notes for real. I can do it. I've done it before. Listen to what Doc Salt and Pepper is saying. Starting right now.

"Well, ladies and gentlemen, that'll do it for class today. I'll see you here on Wednesday. We'll have a quick quiz on today's lecture and then we'll start getting seriously into the text. Make sure you've got yours by then and if you need help preparing for the quiz, I suggest you make friends with that gentleman near the back taking such copious notes. What is your name?"

"Dave Morehead."

"Mr. Morehead, you're about to become very popular. See you on Wednesday."

The First Blow Out Evening

Rhetoric Assignment #1
An Example of Group Dynamics
By Dave Morehead

The First Blow Out Evening was held at Raves's house in the late summer of 1976. His parents were out of town and we were supposed to be over at 8:00 p.m. sharp, though Raves told me to come over anytime I wanted. I got there just after 7:30 and he was powering down a bowl of soup.

"So I'm really excited about tonight," I said by way of hello.

Raves tilted his head and slurped with determination while nodding and impressively not spilling a drop. We had good reason to be excited. We were going to hear hours of music at top volume and neither of our girlfriends was going to be there. Things had not been sailing smoothly in our relationships and we both badly needed a night with the boys.

But at that moment, I was most excited about having a little alone time with Raves. I valued listening to him talk about music. We had similar tastes and that served as the basis, but it was his knowledge of details—especially regarding musicians, producers, instruments, and components—that was most valuable. If I saw an instrument, device, or piece of gear that looked interesting, I could call him for the actual specs, a sampling of consumer opinions, and, in most cases, his firsthand knowledge from either listening to or trying a product.

As was the ritual in those days when one friend visited another, Raves looked through the albums I brought with addictive curiosity.

"Oh great, you brought this," and he held up *Io Sono Nato Libero* by the Italian band Banco Del Mutuo Soccorso. "How is it?" he inquired.

I immediately replied, "Excellent," even while knowing I'd be returning it for money the very next day.

Raves picked up Gentle Giant's *Free Hand* and announced, "This is a great album. Too bad the sound sucked so bad for their show in Santa Barbara."

I could not have agreed more. In fact, with the exception of the drive home, where I got stoned and was given head by Breeana in the backseat of Stein's car, everything had been a disaster that day. My girlfriend was pissed at me and decided not to go to the concert, leaving me to scramble for a ride at the last minute.

I asked Raves, "So how's your love life?"

He reached for my domestic copy of *Voyage of the Acolyte* by Steve Hackett and compared it to his import copy while responding, "What love life?"

We both laughed and he added, "But the way things have been going lately, it's either gonna be my turn or Rod's to have at Bree."

While drawing his attention with a thumbs-up toward PFM's *Photos of Ghosts*, I laughed, "Yeah, what's that about? When did she decide to become community property?"

Raves shrugged and smiled. "At least it's not just men she's fucking," he chuckled while studying *The First Seven Days* by Jan Hammer and then enviously grabbing my mint import of *Red* by King Crimson. "We're definitely getting into this tonight," he proclaimed.

"But this," I stated while furiously digging. "I believe this might do rather nicely as well," and I slid my import copy of *Another Green World* by Brian Eno under Raves's nose.

He gazed at that disc longer than he had any of the others to that point, until tentatively holding aloft *In Praise of Learning* by Henry Cow and asking, "I wonder if we'll be in the mood for this later?"

"Maybe," was all I could muster while hoping we'd pass out before anyone expressed a desire to battle through that challenging piece of vinyl. I only brought mine to show I had it.

"So when are you finally going to leave home?" Raves asked while briefly glancing at *Silent Corner and the Empty Stage* by Peter Hammill.

"As soon as I can. But it's going to take a year or two of saving money. I'm so tired of my parents' bullshit and not being able to play my music loud, and I'm fucking sick of LA," I replied while placing my copy of *Hero and Heroine* by the Strawbs close to the front of my stack.

Raves nodded and said nothing while positioning a pile of his albums on top of the mantel above the turntable. None of what I'd just said was new to him. The doorbell rang and he said, "Don't look through these, yet." As he moved toward the door, he added, "I've got some things in there that are gonna blow you away."

I realized I was having such a great time that I was a little sorry anyone else was coming over. But that feeling was quickly replaced with delight when Lou came in with boxes under his arms and Rod followed with a case of Mickey's Wide Mouth. This was a smart and considerate choice of beverage, not just for the guests, but also for the host house. With a wide mouth, if the bathroom was occupied, you had the comfort and security of using the empty bottle.

"Where'd you get the money for beer?" I inquired, because Rod hadn't worked in almost two years.

He smiled sheepishly. "From the same place I get my good looks," which meant his parents, and I returned the smile. I knew what that was like.

Raves took the boxes Lou was carrying and began examining them on the couch. I placed side one of *Hergest Ridge* by Mike Oldfield on the turntable and announced, "Well, we might as well get started."

Raves proclaimed, "Oh yes, you guys brought some great things," while holding aloft none other than the bootleg of Yes at the Forum, when they performed *Tales From Topographic Oceans*. This was the bootleg with Jon Anderson on disc two introducing "The Ancient," and a member of the audience is clearly heard saying, "I don't want to hear it."

The long first chord of *Hergest Ridge* cascaded through the room and even at a relatively low volume, the sound was massive. Rod anticipated my look of astonishment and announced, "Of course, tonight we're using the Uphonic Vortex System of sound enjoyment."

I laughed and clutched my copy of the first Jade Warrior album while asking, "What the fuck is the Uphonic Vortex System?"

Raves admonished, "Never mind that; the Uphonic Vortex System simply is," and he hurled a copy of *Unorthodox Behaviour* by Brand X at Lou, who responded by flinging a copy of *Pyragony X* by Amon Duul II at Raves. You just had to love Lou. He was a Jew, but he loved those German bands.

We had just opened our first beers when the doorbell rang again, but before anyone had a chance to answer, the door swung open and revealed none other than Breeana. She charged into the room and directly onto Rod's lap dramatically announcing, "Rod,

Rod, surely you must know how incredible it is for me to see you right now."

I glanced at Raves with a look that said, *Oh well, guess it's not your turn yet, old buddy.* But he seemed to have already gotten the message and was contentedly sucking down his brew while browsing the second box of albums.

Bree approached me gushing, "Surely, surely, you know how fabulous it is to see you."

Having looked in the mirror prior to coming over, I replied confidently, "Of course I do."

I grabbed *Selling England by the Pound* by Genesis, pointed to the song "More Fool Me," and said with mock seriousness, "That could have been us, baby."

"Oh darling, darling, that's such a you thing to do," she guffawed, rubbing my head like a favored retriever as she walked on. I'd already had my turn with her, so a hug was out of the question.

On second glance, perhaps Raves wasn't doing so well with Bree's inattention. He'd abandoned the albums and seemed absorbed in a *Better Homes and Gardens* I'd seen on his living room coffee table for at least two months. Breeana stood and stared at him, but Raves kept his head down. She approached slowly saying, "Is that you over there? Is that who I think it is?"

Raves looked up casually and said, "Oh, hi Bree," but his passivity gave way under the avalanche of that woman as she flung herself into his lap. I might have counted him out too soon.

I looked at Rod, who was holding *Fish Out of Water* by Chris Squire and staring at nothing in the middle of the room. Then Lou came back from the kitchen and said, "Well, hi Bree."

Just that fast, she was out of Raves's lap and moving toward Lou, proclaiming, "Lou? Is that Lou baby?"

Despite Lou's never having been a "baby" to anyone except his mother in his entire life, he acknowledged, "That's me."

Bree gave him a peck on the cheek and quickly withdrew because, after all, he'd had his turn with her as well.

"Listen guys," she announced, as if we had a choice. "I've had a simply fabulous time seeing all of you, but I've got to be off."

"Bye," I said.

"Later," Raves bid halfheartedly.

Lou shrugged, sat down, and looked for something on which to place his beer. There was nothing handy, so he grabbed his copy of *Power and the Passion* by Eloy—an album everyone despised—and generously placed it on the coffee table as a coaster for the remainder of the evening.

Rod was not content to settle in for the night just yet, so he sprang from his seat and headed out the front door, shouting, "Wait up, Bree."

It was Raves's turn to shrug. I picked up *Relayer* by Yes and raised one eyebrow in his direction.

"Oh yeah, definitely. 'The Gates of Delirium,'" Raves concurred enthusiastically, but added, "Just let me get another beer first."

"Make it two," I requested.

"Three!" Lou shouted.

Within minutes, Raves and I were standing in the middle of the living room, singing at top volume whatever the hell those lyrics were. We had no clue what any of Jon Anderson's gibberish meant, but we assumed it was something heavy. Raves turned up the volume to a penetrating level while Lou held aloft *I* by Patrick Moraz with one hand and air drummed furiously with the other.

Through the living room window, I could see Rod pleading his case to Bree by the driver's side door as she attempted to make her getaway. The lyrics gave way to the cacophonous, if trebly, instrumental section and the high end was almost excruciating. Raves began playing air bass and I did the best I could with keyboards. Lou continued drumming, by now using both hands.

"Goddamnit!" I shouted. "We need guitar."

"Not anymore!" Rod triumphantly yelled as he burst through the front door, flushed with the aftermath of a successful blowjob.

"That was quick," I yelled, noticing Bree's car was gone.

"What can I say?" Rod shouted. "You're right. She's a hose monster."

"Shut up and play guitar!" Raves roared with both excitement and a little jealousy. But the envy did not last any longer than it took for Rod to pick up his imaginary axe, strap it on, and begin playing with far more precision and knowledge than I could muster on keyboards. Finally, the mellow closing section approached and we were not in the mood to hear Jon Anderson for the rest of the night. Rod and I collapsed on the couch and Raves took the lead by putting on *Larks Tongues in Aspic* by King Crimson.

Markus walked in without saying hello and slipped into place on a chair next to the couch, sliding his own box of albums on the floor in between the couch and coffee table.

He nodded to everyone and we nodded back as we began hungrily rummaging through his discs.

"Oh my God," Raves shouted, holding at least five extremely rare Beatles bootlegs.

Markus grabbed *In the Region of the Summer Stars*, the brand new debut album by the Enid and declared, "This goes on next."

I silently cursed myself for not having a blank cassette handy to record the album. I pointed at *Royal Bed Bouncer* by Kayak in Markus's box and announced, "That should go on after the Enid."

No one heard me or no one cared to react, so I returned to the newly arrived discs, when suddenly Lenny, Manny, Eugene, and Stein joined us.

Markus put on the next album as everyone got beer. When I returned to the living room, I noticed Phil and Randy Ready were newly arrived. Randy held a half full bottle of plum brandy and even as he dramatically swayed, I knew there was at least a 75 percent chance he'd eventually vomit the better portion of that bottle somewhere in the house, and a better than 90 percent chance it wouldn't be a toilet or sink. We all sat down, bringing in chairs from the dining room, or simply planting ourselves on the carpet. Conversations were attempted at a shout, because Markus turned the amplifier to near deafening volume. But what could be heard sounded something like this . . .

"Hey, what's this?"

"It's the Enid."

"The who?"

"The Enid."

"Did he say it's almost over?"

"Let me see it."

"The sound system is great."

"What?"

"It's the Uphonic Vortex System."

"Oh wow."

"What?"

"I have no idea. I'm getting some beer."

"Grab a couple of six-packs while you're in there."

"Who brought the weed?"

"Has anyone heard *Time and Tide* by Greenslade?"

"No."

"No."

"No, but I think everyone has it."

"Excellent, a rolling machine."

"Have you heard *Delayed* by Algarnas Tradgard?"

"Are they German?"

"No, Swedish, I think."

"Fuck that."

"Have you heard *Mr. Mick* by Stackridge?"

"Didn't George Martin produce it?"

"I brought *Expresso* by Gong."

"I think everyone else did, too."

"Isn't Oldfield's lead amazing?"

"His leads all sound the same to me."

"Oh I know, isn't it amazing?"

"Have you puked yet?"

"What is this?"

"What?"

"The Enid."

"What's on next?"

"I brought the surprise."

"You mean, you brought . . ."

"That's right."

"What did he bring? What did you bring?"

"You'll see later."

"Roll some more joints, man."

"Has anyone besides you ever heard *The Lord of the Rings* by Bo Hansen?"

"Probably Bo Hansen, I guess."

"When is Bree coming?"

"All the time."

"What?"

"She was here earlier."

"Is she coming back?"

"If she knows what's good for her."

"What?"

"Did you see the plum brandy?"

"Yeah, you know what that's gonna smell like later?"

"Giggles is here."

"Jesus, is it loud enough for you?"

"No, there's not enough bass. Turn up the fucking bass."

"The bass is loud enough. It's the Uphonic Vortex System."

"What did he say?"

"I think he said it's the Uphony Bullshit System."

"Yeah, that's what I mean."

"MORE BEER!"

"Keep the joints moving."

"Fuck man, this one's wet."

"Have you heard this?"

"What?"

"Have You Heard This?"

"This?"

"What?"

"Wait A Minute, COULD YOU TURN IT BACK DOWN?"

"I THOUGHT YOU WANTED IT LOUDER."

"NO, THE OTHER VOLUME WAS FINE, I GUESS."

"Thanks."

"This is the Enid."

"I'm glad it's almost over."

"Where's your girlfriend?"

"Not here."

"Excellent."

"Are there any girls here?"

"Bree came earlier."

"Bree's always coming."

"How come you say this is the ending, when it just goes on and on?"

"It's the Enid, not the ending."

"Dude, I must be fucked up."

"Uh-oh, get away from me, man."

Mercifully, the Enid finally ended and it was decided to hear selected cuts rather than entire sides. Details started getting a little sketchy at that point as the beer and weed began to take their toll. But I remember "Out of the Blue" by Roxy Music and "One Night in Paris" by 10cc, and we reached another volume crescendo that almost ended the party during "Utopia Theme" from *Todd Rundgren's Utopia*. Many did leave when Lenny insisted on large portions of *Lumpy Gravy* by Frank Zappa. Though this piece managed to at least partially clear the room, those who left all agreed it was amazing. A few more songs followed, the most notable being "Muddy Mouse/Muddy Mouth" by Robert Wyatt, "Claire de Lune" by Isao Tomita, "Lunar Sea" by Camel, and a bootleg cassette I'd made from the second row in the Santa Monica Civic Auditorium of the Tangerine Dream concert they did in conjunction with Laserium. The sound quality of the bootleg was mediocre at best due to the recorder having been on the floor to keep it concealed, but we'd all been there and I was given high marks for making the recording and risking being thrown out. I purchased the cassette recorder with the built-in condenser microphone especially for the occasion. The microphone only lasted about thirty minutes before being completely destroyed by the subwoofers used by Tangerine Dream.

Finally, Raves said to Markus, "I think it's time."

Markus smiled and asked Rod and Lou, "Do you guys think it's time?"

Rod said, "Definitely."

Lou was pretty much blotto at that point, but still had the wherewithal to announce, "Sorry guys, count me out on the circle jerk."

Everyone laughed, but Raves said with disgust, "Oh fuck you, man."

Markus got up and said, "Okay, it's time."

From the closest bathroom, we heard Randy Ready yell, "Hey, wait for me." Then he reentered the living room with a leaning gate, wiping his mouth on his shirtsleeve.

Raves looked surprised and hopeful as he asked, "Did you make it to the bowl?"

Randy smiled and nodded and the entire room broke into applause amid shouts of "All right Randy" and "Excellent, bro."

Only Lou found the cloud when he said, "Wish you could have done that at my house. Instead, you puked all over my mint copy of *Mein Kampf*."

I said, "Lou, that book should be puked on."

Everyone laughed in agreement, and we remained thrilled by the excellent accomplishment of Randy Ready.

Marcus held up his hand in silence and placed into the cassette machine a rare live bootleg of Genesis in 1973, performing their epic "Supper's Ready." He said the recording was of stunning quality and was worth trading one of his duplicate Beatles bootlegs for it. Conversation would have been sacrilegious at that point, so most of us closed our eyes and listened. We had to kick Lou a few times because he started snoring, and someone placed a tissue on the floor next to Randy's mouth because he was drooling. But other than those moments, the room was still and attention was rapt.

When the piece ended, there was a fairly long pause as we tried to gather our superlatives for one more onslaught. But when Rod finally and definitively said, "Well all right," we knew the evening had reached and passed its peak. Selections after that could be classified in the also ran category, and the Uphonic Vortex System was never louder than conversational volume. Even so, there wasn't much conversation as people began leaving while claiming we would have to do this again soon. Within the hour, there only remained Rod, Raves, and me, along with about fifty empty cans and bottles. I placed *Wish You Were Here* by Pink Floyd on the turntable, while Raves opened his dad's liquor cabinet and then the three of us got into the good stuff.

Mr. Morehead,

I enjoyed this. I really did. I can't say I know many of these bands, but that wasn't the point of the assignment. It took me awhile to "get" what you were doing, but after a couple of drinks, I was fine. This is a unique treatment of the assignment, An Example of Group Dynamics. Congratulations. You get an A for the paper. Also, this was especially effective when you read it aloud. Have you considered trying out for the debate team? A word of caution though . . . be careful how you portray women. Cretins don't usually last very long around here.

Dr. Hamer, Phd

A Laundry List of Love

I definitely could have gone for the window-peeking blonde, Jennifer, but she was already involved with someone in the armed forces. I gave it my best shot. We went out a couple of times and had a great kiss. But I couldn't compete with a steady income and a full benefit package. She had the softest hair I ever touched.

I was right about the redhead. Her name was Gwen and she had been plowed, by both genders. She told me she leaned toward women. I told her we had that in common and we became friends. We had an almost moment at a party once when she dared me to tell her something surprising and I admitted how much I thought about her nipples. I asked her to reciprocate with a surprise of her own, and she said my comment was making her soak through her panties.

Maureen was a student in Recreation and Leisure Studies, which is still my favorite name for a major. Essentially, that meant she wanted to become a park ranger—and she had the pit hair to prove it. Initially, it was her face and lack of underwear that attracted me. She was also very clever with a blow-dryer and won a bet from me concerning whether you could successfully fuck inside a Volkswagen Beetle. She had a penchant for sex in public, and, as such, forever changed my opinion of women not being as sexually aggressive as men. My personal favorite was when she blew me during a driving rainstorm under a brown plastic tarp in the stands of venerable and aptly named Cox Stadium, during the third quarter of a football game between State and I have no idea. She had a sometimes boyfriend who was a pot grower in Humboldt County, and I was merely a way to periodically kill some time until she graduated and got an internship with the Park Service. In that regard, she was damn near perfect.

Jocelyn was a student in my department and she made a bet with her friend that a white man couldn't bring her to orgasm. She lost the bet three times.

Sherrice was Jocelyn's friend and she needed verification. Twice.

Dawn was someone I'd gone to high school with and I ran into her at a street fair when she was in San Francisco visiting her brother and his family. She'd thrown up in my lap once and we made out another time. We had both regretted not having a condom that night. So we made up for it after the street fair.

Hun Yi or Hunny, as I called her, enjoyed sex and was really good at it. She was a waitress at one of my favorite cheap restaurants in the Sunset district and a part-time student at State, but unfortunately she still lived at home. We got along pretty well, but I wasn't ready to hang out with anyone's parents, or get serious in a relationship. Plus, neither of us had a car, and we lived in opposite ends of the city, so it was tricky to see her alone for very long. She was sweet, loving, and generous, both with her body and her restaurant's Mu Shu Pork. I hate to admit it, but I hurt her. I never felt like we were going together, but it sure felt like we broke up. Though she never said it, I think she loved me. I never led her on, but she stopped speaking to me after I told her that even though I liked her a lot, I wasn't ready to stop seeing other women. She only went to State one year. I think about her sometimes when I'm alone.

Madeline, or just plain Mad, was a psycho bitch. Ironically, she was also a Psychology major. Gwen warned me about her. She told me that if I was ever stupid enough or desperate enough to go to bed with her, I should wear two condoms at least, and have a splint ready for my penis. There were rumors her last boyfriend had quit the football team, left school, and changed his name. I never went out with Mad, but I smiled at her once—only a day before Gwen told me about her—and she briefly pursued me like a virus. It was difficult to resist at first, because she had a pinup body, but there was something in her eyes that made me feel the circuits were not all properly connected. Thankfully, it only took about a week for her to realize I was a dead end and she turned her attention elsewhere. But just before she did, I truly felt hated.

Soon after that, Amanda made her brief and terrible re-entry into my life. It is difficult to write about her because at one time, we were in love. What happened between us is something that brings me shame. She came to our high school for the last semester and we struck a friendship at first glance. It was a whirlwind. It was also fueled by the knowledge that she was moving out of California a little over a week after we graduated. She was beautiful, but there was more to my attraction than that. It was the first time in my life that I felt a deeper connection with a woman. It was also the first time I'd allowed myself to feel pain. I didn't want her to go and she wanted to stay. We lost our virginity together two nights before she left, atop an open sleeping bag on a miraculously empty stretch of Malibu beach. Afterward, we cried in each other's arms. When she left, I hurt. I also decided it was going to be a long time before I allowed myself to be that vulnerable again.

Over the years, we did manage to correspond from time to time and it was obvious the spark was still there. I wrote her poetry sometimes and I could also be pretty gross. She enjoyed both. She was randy in her letters as well, and the only picture I got of her during that time we were apart was a photocopy of her butt cheeks. When I moved to San Francisco, I pinned the picture to my bedroom wall. In March, I got a postcard from her informing me she'd moved back to LA and wanted to visit. It had been almost three years since we'd seen each other. She gave me her phone number and we spoke for almost two hours. We agreed she should come, and she caught a Greyhound bus three days later. I was so nervous as I walked to the bus station. I was also so happy. My roommate knew who was coming and he cleared out for the weekend. He had no desire to be around for a lovers' reunion and said there wasn't enough cotton in the world he could stuff in his ears. He headed for friends in Monterey and a visit to The Sea. So I was nervous, light of step, and deliriously happy. It was the strangest feeling. It was like my life was beginning again, or perhaps was finally beginning. I also knew that I'd become vulnerable once more and that this visit might have a huge impact on my future.

	I watched every person get off that bus and tears formed in my eyes. I felt silly. I felt wonderful. So when I heard her voice and she was magically standing right in front of me, it is difficult to explain my confusion when I did not recognize her. She'd gained at least fifty pounds. Her once stunning sun-streaked auburn hair was jet black and cut to resemble Mo of the Three Stooges. Except for her voice, there was barely a physical trace of the woman I was expecting to see. I was shocked and didn't know what to say. We awkwardly hugged. I grabbed her bags and we began walking while my mind reeled. Finally, after several uncomfortable seconds and long strides while she struggled to keep up, Amanda grabbed my arm and told me to give her a proper hug. I did as I was told, but was repulsed when I encountered the girth I had to navigate for my hands to meet on the other side. Then we kissed and I wanted to drop the bags and run. For the next two days, that is essentially what I did. I was cold and indifferent. I managed to find out she'd been working in a doughnut shop for the last two years and that explained a lot. But I could not bring myself to tell her point-blank how her change in appearance affected me. She was hurt and wanted to know why I wouldn't talk with her like I used to, or even like I had on our long-distance phone visits, much less touch her. I lied and blamed it on being hurt by other women and feeling vulnerable. I invented a story about a girlfriend and finding her in bed with an ex-friend of mine. I embellished my lie, and I kept it going for most of Amanda's visit.

	She tried to break through, and told me it was okay, that she was with me and she'd make me better. I would not let her touch me in any way. Except for when we fucked. Yes, we did. If only we had not done that, the damage to her and subsequent guilt for me could have at least been minimized. She insisted we share my bed and I reluctantly agreed. The first night was difficult, as I adeptly avoided her advances and kept a mostly wakeful diligence. But during the second night, when fatigue from the ordeal took its toll and I finally succumbed to sleep, she waited and then pounced on my inevitable, inadvertent morning wood. I wish I could say I resisted, but in the camouflage of darkness, a woman taking me against my will was kind of a turn-on . . . and I proceeded to fuck the fat chick. I know how bad that sounds, but that's what it was. I hated myself while I did it, but I did it anyway.

When it was over and we were lying side by side, with the morning light revealing our naked truths, there was no way I could hide my regret. I got up to take a shower, and a couple of minutes later Amanda followed me. She opened the shower curtain and I told her no, please leave me alone. She was standing there nude in the harsh light of my bathroom and that's when I think she understood. Suddenly she looked so embarrassed, vulnerable, and humiliated. She ran from the room. I continued to shower and ponder what to do next. But when I finally got out, she was gone. I hurriedly went to the bus station and stayed all day, watching every person board each bus heading for Los Angeles, but I never saw her. It was only during my walk home that I checked my wallet and found it empty. I had a couple hundred dollars there before Amanda's visit, in anticipation of taking her to nice restaurants. Instead, we'd eaten all our meals at a coffee shop down the street.

I deduced she must have taken the money and caught a flight back to LA. I went home and then bussed to Gwen's apartment, where I spent that night and most of the next day. I told her everything. Once again, I hurt. Gwen agreed I had been an insensitive dick, and it was unconscionable that I allowed sex, but she refused to let me take the entire blame. She told me that my reaction to Amanda's physical change, however shallow, was at least somewhat understandable. She said it would have been far worse if I'd known in advance, let her come anyway, and then been an asshole. Gwen insisted I needed to forgive myself. We were up that entire night talking, but I continued to feel wretched. She said that I'd been taken advantage of too, and I told her that was an interesting take, but somehow I didn't feel like the victim. It wasn't until Gwen gave me a full-body massage late the next afternoon that the healing process began. When she turned me over and saw my erection, she said it was time for me to go. When I got to my apartment, I called Amanda because I wanted to make sure she got home. She answered the phone and I was able to say I was sorry before she slammed down the receiver.

A few weeks later, Gwen introduced me to Janine, who was a very nice woman and actress in the Theater department. This was another unfortunate encounter that never should have consummated, because it ruined any chance of a friendship with Janine. It probably also ruined any chance to succeed with my true motivation for meeting her, which was that I was hoping she could introduce me to Annette, another woman I'd spotted in the Theater department who absolutely took my breath away. But after Janine and I had our night together in her dorm room, I made the horrible mistake of asking questions about Annette while we lay in post-coital embrace. I was an idiot, of course, and a louse. I deserved every bit of shit she threw at me. I also learned a valuable lesson. Theater majors know how to project. Whether it is the throes of sexual satisfaction, or a monologue of venom and hurt, they are trained to reach the farthest seat in the back row. When I hurriedly left that dorm room with belt still unbuckled and shoes in hand, every person on the floor knew who and what I was.

As I walked through campus toward the bus stop, I vowed to become much more discreet and selective in my romantic endeavors. I think that's also when I realized I needed to change in other ways. This was ironic timing, to be sure, because as I walked and pondered and felt something strangely hopeful enter my world, I suddenly came face-to-face with Donna. The last time I'd seen her was in Santa Monica almost a year and a half earlier when she bicycled away from my home in tears. That was the day she'd visited me while my parents were away for the weekend. She was a senior in high school and I was a sophomore at the local Junior College. We'd been hanging out with each other for a few weeks, but there was nothing remotely serious between us, at least in my mind. The day at my parents' house had started well, but ended badly when I told her I was not willing to wait for her to graduate from high school before we had sex. It was October at the time and that meant waiting until the following June. It also meant having a girlfriend still in high school, having to go to high school parties, having to hang out with her high school friends, having to go to the fucking prom, grad night, all that crap I'd left behind forever. As much as I liked her and as beautiful as she was, I knew it had been a mistake to start dating her. All I wanted with her was to have something beyond platonic fun. So I told her that I didn't want to wait, but I hoped we could still be friends. It was a lame line used in breakups throughout time around the world, but I couldn't think of anything better to tell her. She started crying and left without saying another word. In fact, she never spoke to me again. I was sad to see her go that day and delighted to see her again on campus. I had no idea she was going to State. It turned out she wasn't. But I said hello and while she removed her backpack, I held my arms open to greet her. She slugged me hard enough to make my nose and upper lip bleed for most of the bus ride home. I never saw Donna again.

You Fool

Gwen and I talk a lot, especially on the phone. Since the first of this year, 1979, I've spent more time talking with her than I've spent in total with all my lovers. Of all the women I've ever known and not fucked, Gwen is my favorite. My feelings for her have become deep, and my attraction is obvious (as we both noted after my reaction to her full-body massage the day after the Amanda incident). I think my strong attraction and feelings for her are why she asked to meet me earlier today by Stow Lake in Golden Gate Park. Whatever the reason, I was glad.

I saw Gwen approach from the south end of the lake. Due to the whiteness of her skin, she chooses to remain largely covered during the sunniest portion of the day. She said she has enough freckles already and I told her that was complete nonsense. But today, a gloriously warm day in mid-April, she granted me the privilege of seeing her in a black tank top and blue jeans. She had a black sweatshirt tied to her waist and she was braless. Her luscious strawberry hair was long, wavy, and without binding. She wore black, high-top Converse. She had to be the sexiest woman on the planet. I double-checked my left front pocket for condoms and tried to subdue both an erection and the impulse to leer.

"Stop staring at me, you fiend," she declared with a smile.

"Sorry," I responded, without being the least bit.

She leaned over and gave me a full-lipped smooch. I was surprised. Our lips had not touched before.

"That was nice," I said with genuine appreciation.

"Yes it was," she agreed, while sitting down to my left.

I asked, "So, my place or yours?"

She looked at me with mostly disgust and asked, "Is there ever a time you're not ready to pounce?"

"Of course," I insisted. "Foreplay is fun, too."

Before she said anything, I quickly offered, "I'm sorry. It's just you look great. What's on your mind?"

I knew from an earlier phone conversation that she had things she wanted to say and issues she needed to discuss, but I also knew she would not be pressed. She would bring things up, or not, as she saw fit. This was one of the more interesting, alluring, and maddening things about Gwen. She was in charge, not me. Things would go only as far as she would allow. I've never been attracted to a woman so strong willed. But her strength is a complete turn-on.

Gwen suddenly giggled and asked, "Seriously, have you ever not been able to get it up?"

"This is what you want to know?"

"Uh-huh."

"Well then, the answer is yes. One time. Thanks for reminding me."

"What happened?"

I slightly smiled. "Actually, it was pretty understandable. I'd been drunk the night before, and then I beat off three times the next morning, because I didn't think I had any prospects for the day. But lo and behold, I ran into the roommate of a friend, a woman I'd flirted with on more than one occasion. I was walking along Ocean Beach and I saw her walking toward me from below the Cliff House. We talked for a bit, and then suddenly found ourselves in lip lock. She said it was too far to my house, and there were too many people at her house, so we walked up Geary Boulevard and checked into the Seal Rock Inn. But try as I might, and god knows, try as she did, I just couldn't keep it up. It was like a leaky balloon. As soon as she'd blow it up, away it would go. She blamed herself, I blamed myself, and it was all very embarrassing."

"So what did you do instead? Did you stay there or go home?"

"We stayed, talked, I got her off, and she tried me again to no avail. Eventually, we fell asleep."

"I'm glad you didn't leave, that you at least stayed and were intimate."

"Well of course. I mean, we paid for the night and I knew all I needed was a little sleep and I'd be good to go. In the morning, we fucked so hard we could hear the maids laughing next door."

Gwen sighed slightly and patted my upper left leg while saying, "That's such a sweet and romantic end to the story. I'm so happy you finally . . . wait a minute. Do you have condoms in your pocket?"

Though somewhat embarrassed, I asked, "Would you rather I not have condoms in my pocket?"

Gwen considered the question a moment before responding, "I would rather you not presume that you'll have reason to use them today."

I defended, "I always carry condoms, unless I know for sure the woman I'm with is on the pill. I don't want any little Daves at this point in my life. I'm not ready for that."

This stopped Gwen in her tracks, in part because I said it with such force and mostly because she knew it was the truth.

I softened my tone. "But Gwen, you can't blame me for hoping."

She nodded.

Finally, she softly said, "I just don't want to be one more conquest for you. I don't want to be anyone's conquest. Male or female. That's happened to me. I don't like the way it feels."

Before I could respond, she added, "Don't get me wrong. I think about you. I probably think about you more than anyone I've met so far. I think about you when I'm alone. I want you to know that."

I said, "I wish you'd do something about it."

"That's why I'm here today, Dave."

I could feel the heat rising up my neck. "I think about you when I'm alone too, Gwen, but it's more than that. I like you."

She looked at me warmly and said, "I'm really glad to hear you say that. But Dave, I know you. You're not ready to settle down."

I protested. "Who said anything about settling down? How about just spending time together, seeing how we are together? We could . . . exchange St. Christopher medals, you know, go steady or something. Let's buy clothes for each other, watch how we chew, get drunk, and take long walks. Especially in the rain."

She was blushing. I thought, *Oh holy shit, she likes me*. At that very instant, I became scared. I knew I could push it. I knew I could probably have her, perhaps that very hour. But my lust was gone and quickly replaced by fear. Gwen was right. I wasn't ready, and not just for her. I wasn't ready for anyone, and certainly not a woman as strong and assured as Gwen. I didn't even know who the fuck I was.

But there was one thing all wrong with the moment. I said, "Gwen, it shouldn't be this complicated. Our communication isn't complicated. The sex shouldn't be, either. We both enjoy sex with other people for the pure sake of pleasure. We talk about it. So I can't understand why we haven't spent time together naked in the dark. We haven't really even kissed yet. That's ridiculous."

Gwen protested. "We did kiss. We kissed when I got here."

"Sorry dear," I said smiling. "That wasn't a kiss. That was a smooch."

She argued, "Well, I beg to differ, that was most certainly . . ."

I grabbed her and kissed her.

When our lips finally released, Gwen admitted, "I stand corrected."

I asked, "So now what?"

She smiled. "Well I guess, like you said, my place or yours?"

I released her and retreated to a straight-back position on the bench. I replied, "Neither. Let's go to Leon's on Sloat for some barbeque, and then across the street to the zoo."

She looked at me incredulously. "What?"

"I'm hungry," I answered honestly.

She began, "But Dave . . ."

I insisted, "No. You don't want to be a conquest and I don't want to be a complication. Not right now, anyway. Let's just hang out today, have fun, and see where it takes us."

Gwen still looked confused. She said, "I don't know whether to be pleased or hurt."

I shook my head and declared, "I hope you're happy we're friends."

With an admiration that was not quite believed, Gwen asked, "When did you become so mature?"

I answered, not entirely facetiously, "As soon as I realized that was the surest way to eventually get you into bed."

Gwen smiled warmly and rubbed my condoms. "There's my Dave."

We had a great day together, one of the best times I've had with any woman to this point in my life. We ate and laughed and electrically touched from time to time, though for the majority of the day, the sexual tension between us was a pleasure and not a conflict. I think we both knew the reprieve wouldn't last, but we were grateful to spend today as close as two can be without expectation or consummation.

At the end of the day, however, long after we'd gone our separate ways, I was alone in my room, and it was dark.

I could have been with Gwen. Fuck, I could have had her. She offered and she was ripe. I would still be with her now. Again and again.

I wanted her with me so much. I pressed myself against the mattress and craved her. I was denied and almost asleep when the phone rang.

It was Gwen asking, "David, are you thinking about me?"

I answered breathlessly, "Yes."

"Are you naked?"

"Yes."

"Me too . . . you want sex with me right now, Dave?"

"I'm on my way."

"No silly, right now."

"On the phone?"

I heard her smile as she asked, "Are you a phone virgin?"

I admitted, "I'd rather be with you."

With mischief, she said, "You had your chance, you fool."

I pleaded, "Don't tell me that's going to be my only chance, Gwen."

"Who knows? But I wouldn't worry about it right now, Dave. I want you to listen to everything I say, and do exactly what I tell you. Trust me. We're going to come together."

Last Chance for the Hippo

I was walking down Van Ness, heading for the Hippo Burger. I was taking the long way home following a beautiful, though somewhat strange afternoon in the Marina. It had been a warm day, but overcast was spreading across the city and because I'd been walking, the gradual briskness of the air was refreshing. I knew I could get a better value and superior tasting meal if I cut over to Polk and went to Wing Lee's, but I ate there so often, and after the walk I was in the mood for something meaty. I also knew if I went to Wing Lee's, I would probably stop at Rooks and Becords and buy something. The guys there were always playing a new album that I would simply have to own, even if it meant going without dinner. I looked in my wallet. I had enough money for a meal but not an album, even a used album. So the choice was fabulous, inexpensive, Cantonese cuisine, or overpriced American standard. Like I said, it was a strange afternoon, so I chose the Hippo. Of course, I knew Hippo Burger cost too much and their food wasn't even that good. In fact, I was disappointed with every meal I ever had there. But I thought I'd give it one more chance. I wanted a damn burger within walking distance of home. I didn't want to bus out to Bill's Burgers on Clement or the Bill's close to State to get it.

I hadn't been home since catching the 6:30 Van Ness bus that morning on my way to school. I was at State early and then spent the afternoon at Crissy Field, intermittently studying and watching people walk the shore alone, with a friend, or with their dogs. It was getting close to finals, so I really did need to study. I managed to do a fair amount, while being pleasantly inspired by the number of attractive women taking an afternoon walk. As the day wore on, I found myself watching people more and studying less. This wasn't due to procrastination or lust on my part. Something unusual was happening. I couldn't help but notice that some of the people walking were also crying. Many of the conversations were punctuated by animated gestures. There were lots of hugs. People were stopping their own walks to comfort others in distress. It's hard to explain, but the energy wasn't right. It was a beautiful May afternoon, but the people I watched seemed consistently oblivious to the stunning scenery around them. There was no way they could be so jaded as to take it for granted. What was causing that much distraction and pain? I was far enough away from the shoreline that I could not hear conversations. I did hear some words, though. I heard "awful" and "unconscionable," and there seemed a tremendous amount of cursing. In fact, by the time I departed, my initial impression of sadness from people was replaced by undeniable anger.

Something must have happened to the hostages in Iran. That had to be it. I almost walked down to the shore and asked someone what was going on, but I figured it could wait until I got home. I had studying to do and I didn't need the interruption. The world was getting weird enough. For goodness sake, Ronald Reagan might be our next president. Things can't get much weirder than that.

So meat was in order. Grilled and charred and garnished with everything I could pile on top. I was on my way to Hippo Burger and I was hungry.

That's when I noticed people running down Van Ness on both sides of the street. I also heard the far away sound of people chanting. It seemed quite a ways in the distance, but it also sounded like a lot of voices. More people were running. Something was going on. I was by the Hippo parking lot. I was ready to go in. I wanted a burger. Two men were sprinting toward me on the sidewalk.

"What's going on?" I yelled as they approached.

"It's a riot!" one of them yelled back and kept running past.

So I followed and it wasn't long before I reached the crest of Van Ness and saw what was happening. Even from a distance of many blocks, it was obvious things were burning down by City Hall. What the fuck?

There was a huge crowd. People were throwing things and cars were being tipped and set on fire. Except, those weren't just any cars. They were police cars. I could see the red lights reflecting in nearby flames. It looked like at least twenty cars and maybe more were burning. People were throwing things. There was chanting and screaming.

A constant, growing mass joined us in the sprint down Van Ness. As I ran, I asked, "What the fuck is going on?"

Someone yelled, "White got off."

Oh shit. The verdict. What? White got off? That could not be.

I asked, "White got off?"

"Yeah."

Someone else said, "The fucking murderer got off. City Hall's burning down."

It didn't look like City Hall was burning down, but there was bad craziness in the distance and getting closer by the step.

I was confused. Dan White got off? Acquitted? That wasn't possible. He'd confessed to the murders of two men: San Francisco mayor George Moscone and Harvey Milk, the first elected, openly gay supervisor in the history of our nation. Then I started hearing other people talking about manslaughter. Finally, I approached a man who was speaking with several others and I understood what the actual verdict had been. White hadn't gotten completely off, but the verdict was not murder in the first degree. Voluntary Manslaughter? Are you kidding me? White's attorney had argued, among other things, that his client had "diminished capacity" from clinical depression, and in the days leading up to the murder, he'd eaten too many Twinkies, along with other junk food. The press called it the Twinkie Defense. People had openly laughed at the defense argument. They were not laughing anymore.

So what I first thought is that we had a riot by what appeared to be the entire gay community. Even from a distance of two blocks, it looked like most of the rioters were male, but not all of them. Then I realized I couldn't actually tell they were all gay. I was struck at that moment by the assumption I'd made. In fact, thinking back on it, I'm pretty certain there were lots of straight people in the crowd. They were anybody and everybody. I heard and watched grown men and women shouting and screaming in agony and outrage. I felt their pain, yet I was still somewhat detached. I have never been a crowd joiner or conformist. But tonight at City Hall, I finally joined in. I didn't contribute to the destruction, but I lent my voice to the chants and I felt the power and righteousness of the crowd. The only other overt thing I did was throw a perfect cross-body block into a policeman who was about to use his flashlight to hit a defenseless man already on the ground. I'm surprised I did it, but as soon as I put that cop down, I got the hell out of Dodge. I had no desire to incur the wrath and revenge of San Francisco's finest. I ran almost the entire way home on pure nervous energy.

I followed the events for a little while on television. My roommate was away visiting his family. I was not only full of adrenaline from the experience; I was beginning to feel intense sadness. I was both drawn and repulsed to watch and listen as events were described. I felt guilty I wasn't still there and yet relieved to be home and safe. I wanted to break something, and I wanted to cry.

I called Gwen. She had just walked in her door and said she'd been at City Hall as well. In fact, she was more involved than me. She joined the crowd that marched from the Castro District down Market Street. She finally retreated with some of the same group, ever mindful of police reprisal. There were others with her at her place, and I heard their excitement in the background.

We exchanged tales and my cross-body block drew a huge round of cheers from those assembled at Gwen's when she relayed the story.

"I wish I was with you," I said to her.

"Dave, what's the matter?"

"I don't know. I feel sad and confused. I was going to the Hippo Burger for dinner, and then all this happened."

She said, "Dave, a lot of people feel like that right now. I've got a house full of people that are pissed and sad and confused. Something terrible happened today and no one knows what to do next. I feel exactly like them. So unless you can be a little more specific about yourself, unless you really need me right now, maybe we should just talk tomorrow."

"Okay," I said meekly and hung up.

I was miserable. The emotion was impacted by events of the day, for sure, but it wasn't only the inconceivable verdict that prompted what I was feeling. I knew this had been building up in me over a period of months, gathering force, taking shape. Something was changing in me. It was confusing and painful and this wasn't the first time I found myself wallowing in it. My most recent journal is so full of it, I'm considering throwing it away. No one will ever be allowed to read it.

Less than a minute after I talked to Gwen, the phone rang.

"You hung up on me," she said with surprise and a little anger.

"I'm sorry. I thought we were done," I replied, which was true.

"Dave, what the fuck is wrong with you?"

"Gwen, why are you mad at me? You said we'd talk tomorrow."

"I'm not mad at you," she stated, while still sounding angry. Then she added, "Dave, everything is completely crazy right now. I feel like the whole world has gone nuts."

"I feel like I'm a little nuts right now, too."

Gwen scolded, "Goddamnit, Dave, get out of yourself. The world doesn't revolve around you and your shockingly narrow concerns."

The room was spinning. I hadn't felt like that since being caught in a lie by my parents. I also felt Gwen was being unfairly harsh, but at the same time, there was wisdom in what she was saying. For perhaps the first time in my life when under personal attack, I did not respond defensively or counterattack.

"Gwen, I know it doesn't revolve around me. I know that. I've never felt so small and stupid. I've been feeling that way a lot lately. I . . ."

"I, I, I, I, how many more times are you going to say I?" Gwen assailed. "I'm with people right now that are concerned with we, not I. They're thinking about everyone, not just themselves. Jesus Dave, I know you're an only child and this is what you're used to—your life, your needs, your dick, the things you write— everything has always been about you. But it's when you get outside yourself that I like you most. I probably love you. But I don't love who you are at this moment. You need to get out of your own way."

"How do I do that?" I asked.

"You're the only one that can answer that."

"Gwen, I'm sorry I'm being such a . . ."

"Self absorbed loser dick?"

That comment pissed me off, but I managed to respond, "Okay. Sure. That'll work. So then, what can I do to help?"

"That's up to you, babe. I don't know. Go to the Castro and find someone that needs a hug. There's a rumor the cops are coming for revenge. You're a big guy. Lend a hand. Write something. Write a letter. I don't know. Figure it out. Dave, I've got to hang up. There are others that need me right now. Can I let you go?"

"Yes."

"You're sure?"

"Yep."

"Do you really mean that?"

"Uh-huh."

Gwen sighed and then said, "Everything I said earlier, and you're okay with that?"

"Absolutely."

"That's all you have to say?"

"Yes."

"Are you mad at me?"

"No."

"Why won't you talk with me?"

"You said you have to hang up."

"Is this some fucking trip you're playing with me?"

"Gwen, when I tried to talk with you, I got attacked and told how selfish I'm being. You told me you have to go, because you have people there that need you, so now my short answers aren't expansive enough. What do you want from me? You can't control my reactions. They're for me to work out, know what I mean?"

"I'm sorry. I'm just so upset. I guess I was being . . ."

"You were trying to be a good friend, though it came out a little bitchy."

"You're right. Thank you."

"Thank you too. Now with your permission, I'd like to either find something constructive to do to make this day better, or I'd like to deal with my own shit in my own way."

"I really do love you."

"Okay."

"I can let you go now? You're all right?"

"Yes. I'm just hungry."

"You could probably go get your burger now."

"I'll never eat at the Hippo again. That's where the guy I used to be ate."

"That's nice to hear. Good night, Dave."

We hung up and I spent about two minutes thinking about what I'd like to do. I really was hungry. So I called Maureen, who had recently gotten her internship and would be leaving the Bay

Area over the summer. She said she'd pick me up in half an hour, because she was also in the mood for something meaty.

"More people have been slaughtered in the name of religion than for any other single reason. That, my friends, that is true perversion." —Harvey Milk

Jesus and Me

The name of the class is Sex Roles in Communication. Gwen insisted I take it. Since it is an elective and sounded interesting, I did. The class is being taught by one of the leading lesbian activists in the city and when I heard that, it screamed red flag to me. But Gwen told me the professor was a wonderful teacher and the experience would be good for me. I asked her what she meant by "the experience" and she simply smiled and told me that typically, the ratio of women to men in that particular class was about ten to one.

Gwen added, "How can a guy like you resist odds like that?"

I love Gwen. I also miss her. She left State after the spring term and by the fall of 1979, she had moved to Portland, Oregon. Her sister lives there and recently had a baby. Gwen wanted to be close to help. She is continuing her education at Portland State. Before leaving, however, she made me promise to take this class.

She is entirely wrong about the ratio. It is twenty-seven to one. I am the only male. There was briefly one other man. His name is Tim Yu, and he didn't say much. He is a Business major needing communication credits and this is one of the classes he chose. With all due respect to Tim, who seems or seemed like a nice guy, I am alone now. It is me against them. I am to bear the sins of all mankind against the wrath of women. It is probably going to be a rout. Gwen was right about the professor, Dr. Monica Lewin. She is tall, with short cropped gray hair shaped in a sort of wedge cut that many lesbians seem to prefer. She has a commanding and almost intimidating presence. But when she speaks, she seems like a nice woman and were it not for her and one of the supportive women in the class, I probably would have dropped it after today's session. Because I was in the midst of the frying pan this afternoon, I didn't have time to take any notes, so I will attempt to reconstruct the events from the immediacy of memory. It won't be exactly as it happened, but as I'm likely to never forget this day, it's liable to be pretty close.

It started innocently enough. We were instructed to put on name tags and introduce ourselves, state our major and briefly explain why we were taking the class. I felt intimidated by the number of women. This was a brand new feeling for me. Part of it came from the numbers, but I also noticed how some women stared at Tim when he spoke. When a few of them caught my eye, they seemed to glare at me with something less than warmth. The vibe was not pleasant. It might have only been a few that were causing this feeling, but it was palpable. I've never felt like that in a classroom before. There was no incident, however, during the introductions.

Then, Dr. Lewin asked, "What are each of us raised to believe about what society expects from us? What do we expect from ourselves? What limitations does society place on us? What limitations have we already placed on ourselves? What is a woman? What is a man?"

I have never felt less inclined to speak than at that moment. I sensed anything I said would be subject to attack. As Dr. Lewin asked her last question, I understood exactly why Gwen wanted me to take the class. I thought, *You fucking sneaky bitch*, and I couldn't help but slightly giggle out loud.

That's how it began. I was chuckling at what my very good, bisexual female friend told me. Oh, the irony.

"What the fuck are you laughing at?" demanded a dyed blonde mullet-haired woman named Connie two seats to my left.

"Something a friend said to me about this class."

"And what was that?" another woman from behind asked challengingly.

"**She**," I emphasized the word, "told me that taking this class would be a good experience for me."

Dr. Lewin asked, "Dave, why do you think she said that?"

I considered the question a few moments before responding. "I think it's too soon for me to answer that, but I have a feeling I'm about to hear a whole bunch of theories from my classmates."

Dr. Lewin slightly smiled and then asked, "Okay, what do you think Dave's friend meant?"

A woman named Grace, who looked a little but sounded a lot like Edith Bunker said, "Clearly, his friend thinks he could benefit from the feminine perspective."

"And what is the feminine perspective?" Dr. Lewin asked.

There was a slight pause, but it felt like the dam was beginning to break.

A somewhat heavyset, though very pretty brunette woman named Jessica bellowed, "That men are fucking assholes, and have always been fucking assholes, whether they're fucking women, or fucking assholes."

The room erupted in varied reactions, though most were guttural laughs of ribald delight. Even I laughed.

"What the fuck are you laughing at?" asked Connie again while glaring at me.

"It was a funny line," I defended.

"Yeah," Connie continued, "but that isn't the only reason you laughed."

"Oh I see. You're a mind reader, too. Excuse me; have we met before this class? What gives you such keen insight into what I think?"

"You're a man," someone shouted and there was immediate applause and laughter.

At that point I took the bait. I was pissed.

"I see; so then, are all women clairvoyant? Or is that a special power endowed on angry lesbians?"

At that moment, I understood the sort of rage Andy Kaufman provokes when he wrestles women. Several stood up and looked like they wanted to hurt me, and a few were willing to volunteer for the assignment. I believe it was only because Dr. Lewin held up a hand and had such strong influence on everyone that I was not jumped on the spot. As long as I live, I hope to never again face such anger. Honestly, I was frightened.

Dr Lewin shouted, "Ladies, take your seats and remain calm. This is a discussion group, not an avenging horde."

"You could have fooled me," I stated low, but clearly audible.

Dr. Lewin fixed a stern look at me and counseled, "Mr. Morehead, I would advise you to choose your words a little more carefully. Your point of view, however valid it is to you, is clearly in the minority here."

I nodded.

She continued, "Ladies and gentlemen, every point of view is welcome in this class, no matter how inflammatory it sounds at first. Your reactions are also encouraged, but there will be no threats and there will be no retribution other than verbal intercourse. This is how it is going to be and if any of you are incapable of working within this structure, I suggest you leave now. But it is my belief that if you stay, you will **all** benefit from the experience."

She paused at this and the room quieted before she asked, "Dave, when you were growing up, what were you taught at home about the roles of women and men in the world? And ladies, please allow him to answer this question in full."

I took a deep breath and allowed my head to clear a little before answering. "My mom was the typical stay-at-home mother. She was a housewife. Dad made the money."

"Who made the decisions?" asked Dr. Lewin.

"They both did."

"Really?" she questioned.

As soon as she asked that, I realized my answer was not entirely correct. I said, "No, that's not completely right. When Dad made a decision, it was final. When Mom made a decision, sometimes it was final and sometimes she had to check with Dad."

"Typical," someone said with disgust.

Dr. Lewin questioned, "To the best of your knowledge, was it like this in the homes of your friends?"

"Yeah, for the most part."

"Class, does this sound familiar to anyone else in here?" Dr. Lewin asked.

There was a murmur of agreement, but still a lot of tension.

"I had no father when I was growing up," announced a trim and muscular woman named Brenda who sat to my immediate right. "He left when I was two."

"Did you have a father figure in your life?" asked Dr. Lewin.

"Only the men Mom brought home, and, until I got older, all they wanted was to fuck, and drink," admitted Brenda.

"What changed when you got older?" another woman asked.

Brenda sneered, "They wanted to fuck me, too."

"It was the same thing in my house," agreed Connie. "Fucking and drinking and fighting were the only things men wanted to do."

I thought, *But there isn't a drink ever made to make them want to fuck you.*

"Yeah," Grace chimed in. "What's that about? Why are all men so preoccupied with sex? Even when they're kind of nice, I always feel like they're only being that way to get laid."

"Hey, honey," an African-American woman named Marlene gently chided. "I feel like the men sometimes. It isn't only men who are nice in order to get laid."

"Thank you," I said.

"Fuck you," responded Connie.

"No thank you. It's a kind offer, but I'll pass."

"Don't fucking talk to me, shit for brains, and stop looking at my tits!"

"Don't flatter yourself. I'm looking at your name tag."

"Really? Then what's my name?" Connie asked while covering her tag.

"Toro?"

"Mr. Morehead . . ." Dr Lewin began, but before she could continue, a single laugh erupted from the back of the room. It started with a snort and ended with a five HA cackle. It was a huge, obnoxious laugh. It was a wonderful thing to hear. We all turned and it was a shapely, auburn-haired woman named Cynthia. *Nice tits*, I thought.

"What's your problem, sister?" asked Connie.

"You are," Cynthia admonished. "I mean, give the guy a break."

Before Connie could respond, Dr. Lewin stated, "That's enough!"

I turned and looked directly at Connie. I said, "Connie, that was a bullshit thing I said. I'm sorry. But I wasn't staring at your tits."

Connie did not acknowledge the apology, but it temporarily stifled her.

Dr Lewin instructed, "Could we please get back to societal expectations when we were children?"

"You know what's strange?" Brenda asked and then continued. "When I was a girl, I was called a tomboy. I liked playing with guys and they were very accepting of me. Most of the girls thought I was weird. But the guys were okay. It wasn't until puberty that guys started making fun of me for hanging out with them. The girls still thought I was weird. I was never into the stuff they were into. Makeup, fashion, trendy things. My mom thought I was weird, too. I really didn't have a role model, until I moved to San Francisco."

Jessica asked, "Is that when you realized you're gay?"

Brenda said, "I'm not gay. I'm attracted to men and I'm still a tomboy."

Connie smirked, "You **are** fucking weird."

"Girl, give it a rest," Marlene scolded.

Cynthia said to Brenda, "Something that's interesting is that the boys accepted you before puberty. A friend I work with is gay. He was never interested in what other boys wanted to do and they never accepted him. But neither did most of the girls. Everyone, including his mother and father, thought he was weird."

I turned around, faced Cynthia, and asked, "Has he found friends as an adult?"

"Oh hell yes," Cynthia smiled. "San Francisco is heaven for him."

There was a murmur of consent to that statement.

Grace asked, "So could someone please answer my question about why men are always wanting to get laid?"

"Because men are fucking animals," Connie flatly stated. Several women agreed with Connie's assertion.

I was still looking at Cynthia. But I noticed Grace was staring at me and expecting me to answer her question. I glanced at Tim, who had made himself as small as possible while fingering his pencil. I looked around the room and almost everyone was staring at me. I looked at Cynthia again, and she had a mischievous little smile on her face. I looked outside the window into the courtyard separating the hallways of the HLL building and watched a blind man walking with his Seeing Eye dog. That's when it came to me. Connie was right.

I said, "Nature films. That's what it's like. Do you remember seeing sex in nature films? The Jane Goodall stuff. National Geographic presents, 'The Wild Horses of the Rockies,' you know, films like that. Do you remember them? Do you remember how sex is in those films? When does sex happen in those films, or in nature? Is it when the female comes of age, or is it when the male comes of age?"

"The male," answered Cynthia, her smile becoming something more than mischievous.

"That's right," I said smiling back at her, wondering if something had just started between us, and then I continued. "In nature, the very first day a male comes of age sexually, he's probably going to get laid. Or at least, he's trying to get laid. He can't help himself. He can't control it. And at no point does any living thing tell him to stop. In fact, he better hurry up and get to it, or some other creature in his tribe will beat him to it. But for people, for men, when we come of age, when we can't help it or control it, we are told to do exactly that. We're told we have to wait. We're told we have to suppress our natural instincts. We are made to feel ashamed. We can't control the way we feel any more than the ape, horse, or any other male. We're at our sexual peak on day one, and then it only becomes a question of how long we can keep it up."

There were giggles at this.

I continued, "I'm sorry, that wasn't meant as a joke. My point is that, I think the more we are made to suppress our natural instincts, the harder it gets."

Again, there were giggles.

I was starting to feel embarrassed, so I concluded, "I don't know if it's as simple as I just portrayed it. I would never dream to understand how it is for women. I do remember, however, in my high school sex education class, there was a lot of time spent discussing a woman's period and hardly any time at all discussing an erection. And I know a lot of men would agree with what I just said. It's very difficult. It's frustrating. I think, sometimes, that frustration can turn us into . . . like you said, Connie, animals."

I turned around, faced the front, and felt flush. There was a pause, and then several people, including Dr. Lewin, applauded me. When the applause ended, she added, "Thank you, Dave. That was brave and insightful."

Connie spoke up. "Okay, that's great, but before we give him his Boy Scout medal and elect him president, I'd just like it to be known that my sexual desire has also been strong from the start. I don't think men have a monopoly on that."

Marlene added, "That's what I'm talkin' about. I like it. I like it a lot. I want it. I'm tellin' you, when I get home tonight, after this class, my boyfriend's gonna put out or get out."

There was class-wide laughter at this, but something about it bothered me. I said, "That's great, but if I said the same thing about making a woman put out, would I have gotten the same reaction?"

"Probably not," admitted Brenda.

Connie added, "But then, you're an asshole."

"Why do you say that? You don't know me," I challenged.

Connie said, "I've heard about you."

I turned and faced her. "You've heard about me? From who?"

She shrugged and said, "Girls talk."

"Oh that's just fucking great," scolded Cynthia. "Gee Connie, thanks so much for reducing every woman in this room to a stereotype."

"Fuck you, bitch, I'm sick of your shit," warned Connie as she clenched her fists, again looking like she might pounce.

Cynthia would not back down. "Are you threatening me? So what is it exactly that's separating you from the men you lampoon? You're just as bad as you portray them to be. So far in this class, you're even worse."

The room was threatening to ignite.

I glanced at Dr. Lewin, and she was just about to intercede when we all heard, quite clearly, "Stop it, all you stupid people."

It was Tim. My man, Tim. Taking up the good fight because he'd had enough. Damn, I was proud to be a guy. Tim snapped his pencil in half, grabbed his books, got up, and left. That was the last any of us saw of Tim in that class.

"Well, that's two less balls in here," Connie advised.

"Not counting yours, of course," I added.

"STOP!" shouted Dr. Lewin.

"Lord have mercy, this beats the soaps," Marlene said.

A nervous laughter ran through the room. There was a long pause while everyone considered where to go from there.

Dr. Lewin redirected us. "Class, there are a lot of interesting dynamics at play here and much to think about. I suggest we break for the day and allow ourselves the opportunity to reflect. I would also like each of you to write a brief paper summarizing today's events. The paper will not be graded. But it is required if you want to continue in this class. Lastly, I would like to speak with Connie and then Dave in my office. I want to speak with each of you, separately. Connie, if you could come right now and Dave, please be outside my office in half an hour. To all of you, this was an excellent and enthusiastic session. If we can maintain this energy throughout the semester, we have a chance to do some very good work. See you Thursday."

It was a good call. We needed air and space and we weren't going to get any in that room today.

I let the class file out. I was spent. I felt like I'd been in a fight. I literally felt like the last man standing. Tim was gone. If I stayed, it was going to be me and me alone. Well, maybe not quite alone.

Jessica walked past me on her way out and said, "You're still a fucking asshole," though she was smiling when she said it.

"Thank you for sharing," I slightly smiled back at her.

I felt a soft hand on my shoulder and then Cynthia asked, "How you feeling?"

"Beat up."

"Want to get some coffee before you meet with Monica?"

I considered the offer and responded, "I suppose coffee would be better than beer."

Cynthia smiled. "I could go for a beer."

So down to the famous pyramid-shaped student union we walked and soon found ourselves sucking down our beers like survivors of some kind of wreck. We talked about the class. Cynthia got me to admit that just before I began my explanation on the male sexual dilemma, I actually was staring at her tits. She was okay with that. Suffice to say we started a friendship.

My meeting with you, Dr. Lewin, is not really part of this paper. I will say this . . . you and your class are giving me much food for thought. Don't worry; I don't think we'll have a repeat of today. Of course, I can only speak for myself. You say Connie won't be as abusive in the future and I wish you the best of luck facilitating that. Time will tell. But I welcome the challenge. It beats the crap out of most classes I've ever had. And I will think a great deal about what you said. About what can rise from the ashes of demolition, being open to growth, change and possibility, about starting to view myself through the eyes of others, especially those who don't share my point of view. I don't think I have much to worry about in that regard in your class.

One last note, however, that I think you'll find amusing. Maybe you'll find it insulting, I don't know, but I'm going to include it.

I called Gwen tonight and told her everything that happened. She laughed her ass off. I told her the next time I see her, she owes me a grudge fuck.

The Way Things Are

Dr. Lewin, I realize this is not an assignment and you weren't expecting this in your mailbox. But I had to get it off my chest and I don't know where else to go. Whatever my reasons are for giving it to you, I suppose I'm writing this mostly for me.

I don't know. This whole gay thing takes a lot of getting used to. Before I moved to San Francisco, I was told to expect to be shocked. Once I got here, some well-meaning but tiresome straights cautioned me to just wait and see how bad it is, how homos are everywhere. I was at the Off Union Saloon recently with a woman visiting the Bay Area from Baltimore. She was a friend of an old buddy of mine in Los Angeles and he'd given her my number and told her I'd show her around the city. One of her legs was starting to press against mine under the table, when we suddenly overheard two loud and sloppy drunks hunkered at the bar. They were burly blue-collar types at the end of a working day, manly men commiserating about the way things used to be compared to the way things are. One guy said the most amazing thing to him was how the number of homos seems to multiply on a daily basis, even though they can't sexually reproduce. His companion claimed he had it figured out. He said this was finally the end of the great American migration west that started before the gold rush, and began peaking with the building of the transcontinental railroad. They were both pretty smashed, and they ended this historical revelation by clinking their shot glasses, downing them with vigor, and proclaiming, "Faggots Ho!"

There was a smattering of laughter around the bar from some of the locals who agreed, at least in spirit, that things weren't what they used to be. However, I believe I'm safe in saying no one in the bar expected what happened next.

The two drunks turned on their stools to face each other. One of them said, "Oh Charles."

Charles gently touched the face of his companion and tenderly intoned, "Yes, Bert."

Then, they kissed. They kissed like men that meant it. They kissed like they had kissed before. They left a generous tip, and then the bar, arm in arm, still kissing, seemingly anxious to kiss and more.

One of the interesting elements to me in these times is that no one seems to have a major gripe about two naked women. Certainly, I don't. I had the pleasure of a liaison with two women who are bisexual. Trust me, there is nothing like being blown by two mouths, four hands, and four breasts to unleash the full orgasmic potential of a penis. We're talking ceiling shots. Granted, I've heard both men and women make derisive comments about lesbians who are overly butch. But even then, imagining sex between two women is less invasive and far more attractive, except for the strap-on parts.

But two men having sex seems . . . problematic for starters. Who goes first? And when that guy is done, what keeps him from going to sleep before the other guy gets off? And then there is simply the blunt insertion factor. I don't like to think about that. I don't even like it when a doctor inserts a single gloved and lubricated finger up my ass. There's one more thing. This is gross, but as long as I'm purging, I might as well add that I don't like anal odor. I've lost my desire and even some erections because my nose veered a little too close to the bung zone on women just slightly removed from their last washing. Hell, I don't even like the way my dick smells about twenty-four hours after a shower. I respect the women who've told me that I had to wash before they'd swallow.

I know what you'd say about what I just wrote, Dr. Lewin. I'm writing almost purely about sex and you've told me I need to broaden my horizons. I am becoming aware, theoretically at least; relationships are about far more than sex. But, as you bluntly pointed out the other day in class, that I'm only now realizing this is probably why I haven't had a real relationship yet.

But it is sex, pure and simple, that has kept me from understanding a man being attracted to a man. Come to think of it, and this strikes me as ironic, at least from my narrow perspective, I believe a man coming out of the closet is more difficult than a woman doing the same thing. Granted, this is based mostly on my revulsion toward the male sexual acts, but I don't think I'm far off base in saying that a lot of people feel as I do. Regardless, it has been substantially more difficult for me to picture a man with a man than it is to picture a woman with a woman.

All that said, I witnessed some things earlier tonight that have radically changed my perspective. I went to the Castro District. It was my first time there for Halloween. I got there early because I was told by my roommate not to miss a single moment. My impression from his description was that I was going to witness a sort of cultural freak show. He suggested I drop acid. I declined. I did enough of that in the spring of 1978 to last a lifetime. Anyway, I painted half my face and neck completely black, and wore the loudest colored shirt on the planet, which I happened to steal from Gwen before she moved. It was slightly snug on me, but I had to have it. I thought I looked outrageously garish, though my roommate said I'd fit right in.

When I got there, the first place I stopped was outside Cliff's Variety. When I saw the window display, I almost wished that I had used hallucinogens. It was spectacular. There were also many children in costumes, eating pie and magically running around a flatbed trailer parked in front of the store. I never had that much fun trick-or-treating when I was a kid. It seemed that many of these children and their parents viewed this as a tradition. That was an amazing revelation all by itself. Parents were allowing their children in the Castro District, with gay people in costumes sauntering all around them. It was wonderful and so full of joy and innocence. Honestly, I felt a door opening in my heart that I didn't even know existed. Of course, there were a lot of pictures of Harvey Milk and even a few of George Moscone. It was a sad reminder, but the feeling those photos invoked for me was of collective strength forged from all the pain.

Twilight passed into night and the real party began. I've never been to anything like that. Beyond the spectacle, one of the strongest impressions I got was the sense of community. I live in the Marina. It's a beautiful place, but there is no real visible pride in living there, other than the general joy of living in San Francisco. But the Castro is completely different, and I don't think my sense is based solely on the party, or what I was about to witness. I've felt this way before in that district, like when I've seen movies at the incredible Castro Theater, and then window-shopped afterward while eating ice cream. I've felt it since the first time I went there, but only now can I articulate it, and it was this night that brought it all into focus. Of course, I don't have to tell you what it was like. You might have been there. Gwen told me you live in the area. I saw a few people from campus and had drinks with several. Unfortunately, I got drunk. It took several hours and a lot of reveling to get there, but I had too much. I wasn't alone in being drunk, but being straight and that drunk in the Castro is surreal, and sociologically challenging.

I needed to urinate and was a little frightened of using the men's room at the bar, so I staggered outside and then down 17th Street, past Hartford, looking for a bush, gutter, or even a large parked car I could kneel behind and relieve myself. I found a spot between a Mustang and a VW van, dropped to my knees, and commenced. I was in midstream, being delightfully serenaded by the sounds of the street party a block and a half away, when I heard several angry voices in the opposite direction. I peered around the Mustang and saw four men standing over another man who was seated against the Noe Street sign. I was about thirty-five yards from them. They were calling the man faggot with almost every sentence and then I clearly heard one of them say, "Boys, I think this is who we've been looking for."

I've heard about muggings in the Castro. I've also read about them in the *Chronicle*, but I was having a hard time fathoming that this could happen on Halloween night with so many people partying in the area. These assholes must have been lurking on the outskirts, just waiting for someone to be walking alone. I was finished pissing, but almost paralyzed with fright, not even aware that some of the urine trickled toward the curb and soaked into the left knee of my jeans.

One of the standing men broke a bottle against the street sign, the beer and some of the glass raining onto the head of the man on the ground, who pleaded, "No, please don't."

This is life or death, I thought. What to do?

Take a deep breath. Get up. Use your voice. DO SOMETHING! Okay you cowardly motherfuckers, here I come. I quickly rose to my feet.

Just then, I heard a whistle blow about thirty yards away and closing from Castro Street. It was soon followed by another whistle and another, and then still more. Within seconds, I swear, there were men with whistles running full speed down 17th Street. Other whistles could be heard approaching in both directions on Noe and Hartford. There were still more whistles from far away. I had no idea what the fuck was happening. They were running by me. They were all in costume, some in tight-fitting uniforms, and others in long flowing gowns with stoles. One man was wearing a huge turban filled with plastic fruit, and another with almost shoulder-length white opera gloves cradled a giant fox head. There was a short man with a plump little butt, lariat in hand, only wearing chaps, boots, and a cowboy hat. There were bare feet in nylon stockings, high heels, and hard leather. They were all blowing their whistles. The four men that were about to attack the man on the ground had turned and sprinted as fast as they could down 17th Street in the opposite direction.

Within seconds, the bad men were long gone and the good men were helping the victim to his feet. I joined them as they aided the man, whom someone called Jay, who was more frightened than injured, back to the safety of the bar. I drank black coffee and felt both exhilarated at what I'd just witnessed and a little guilty that I had not moved more quickly and been more heroic. Men with whistles had done it for me. Men with whistles. I was profoundly moved and affected by this.

I wanted to do something, say something, thank someone, but the rescuers didn't stick around the bar for long. There was a party still going strong in the street, and whistles might be needed elsewhere. Jay cried and eventually started going into shock. A doctor was called and just before I left, a man dressed head to toe as a female nurse was tending Jay.

So I caught Muni home and eventually wrote this. Maybe I can read it aloud in class. I'm still confused about a lot of things in this world. But there's no going back to the way I was before about gay people. What I witnessed tonight marked me. Those men have come to an understanding and acceptance of themselves that I have not yet achieved. I want to be that comfortable in my own skin. I was right there with them tonight. I was surrounded by full on flaming homosexual men and they were no threat to me at all. I didn't even get hit on. Apparently, I'm not that hot. I told my roommate. I called friends. I became aware that at least a few of them are no longer really my friends. One of them even asked me if I had become gay. Can you believe that?

I really love our class, Monica. It's one of the best I've ever had. I can't believe how I've become friends with some of the women that seemed to hate me. I've even made Connie smile with some of my attempts at self deprecating humor. I've got a crush on about half the women. I just wish there were more men in there, more good men, like homos.

Impulse Shopping

Spring 1980. Greg and Mike were doing their comic thing, along with the rest of the improvisation group, Faultline. They were killing us. I was at their show with a bunch of friends from school, my roommate, and a few of his friends. The cheap red wine was flowing. We were all pretty drunk. I still am as I write this.

I was sitting next to Cynthia, but about three tables across from me was Annette. I'd still never met her. I tried being discreet. But I couldn't stop glancing, observing, staring. Our eyes only met once, but hers twinkled. Was it a smile I saw? Or do her eyes simply twinkle all the time?

I badly wanted to walk over there and introduce myself. I considered that I might completely blow it and maybe even get humiliated. It didn't look like she'd come alone. She didn't look like she ever went anywhere alone. Admirers and friends surrounded her. She would never, in her entire life, have any problem finding suitable companionship for an evening. She probably has a boyfriend. She probably has several others sitting at their homes right now, waiting for the phone to ring and it be she. They're probably all older than me, with full medical and dental. Professional men. Women, too. Cultured. Like fucking yogurt. I'll bet she never drinks the rancid $1.99 shit we were drinking earlier, and that I still may end up puking, now that I'm home.

But back at the show, there I was, trying to muster the courage to introduce myself to the lovely Annette. Trying to stifle an erection that was threatening both local and state borders. How would I manage?

Cynthia was suddenly laughing. I love her laugh. Some people don't. Apparently, one of those people was Greg, who stopped his improvisation, glared at Cynthia, and asked if anyone in the house had a muzzle. I raised my hand.

I turned Cynthia toward me and kissed the living shit out of her. And boy did she kiss back. It was our first kiss. A showstopper. Applause. I guess that sort of sealed the deal with Cynthia and me. When we finally finished and everyone turned his or her attention back to the stage, Annette was gone.

Three fucks in thirty-five days.

      Reagan
      Lennon
      Cynthia

I hope third time is the charm.

So This Is Christmas

John Lennon is dead. John Lennon is dead. Some sick motherfucking piece of shit I will never mention by name shot and killed John Lennon.

The ten minutes of silence were wonderful. Thank you, Yoko. But they were not enough.

Cynthia can't help me, except to say it will get better. I guess we're a couple now. It took a lot of convincing on my part, but we recently started sleeping together. I don't know if either one of us thinks it's a great idea, but we make each other laugh and sex is something I've missed. I also like Cynthia a lot, at times, even though there are some things we don't agree on at all. In truth, the thing that bothers me most is since I started spending nights with Cynthia, Gwen and I don't talk as much as we used to. I miss her so much.

I really feel depressed. I wonder if this is how some people in San Francisco felt when Milk and Moscone were murdered.

People are going on about their lives. Celebrations are being planned. Lights are going up and trees are in windows. I don't have much time to make plans. I go to school and work. That's about it, though I do manage to have some fun at work. I don't even write as much as I used to. Life goes on, but I don't know how to get past this. This is the first death that's truly affected me.

In a few days, I'll fly home for the holidays and see old friends and some of them will talk with me about it, but others have already tired of the subject.

I've made tapes with nothing but his songs and worn them out listening night after night. Even my roommate, who has been very understanding, has asked me to use headphones.

And fucking Ronald Reagan is about to be president. Are you kidding me? How much worse can things get? I've got to do something. I've got to try something. I'm going to play one Lennon song and try to let him go. What song to play? There's an obvious choice, of course. But "Imagine" is something I don't want to associate with his death. "Give Peace a Chance"? Not yet, I guess. Wait, I've got it. I'll play the song the radio station played at sunrise the morning after he died. "Old Dirt Road." I've got the LP.

John Lennon is dead. John Lennon is dead. John Lennon is dead.

So long. Bye bye. Keep on keepin' on.

Work in the Eighties Part 1

"Good evening, ladies and gentlemen. Like always, I'm the only one here tonight. If you want something from the concession stand, I'll help you as soon as I finish selling tickets."

"Why isn't anyone else working?"

"Because the owner is cheap."

"Other theaters have more than one person working."

"I'm glad you noticed that."

"How do you manage?"

"I make people wait."

"But don't they get mad?"

"Sometimes."

"Isn't that frustrating?"

"No, I love being made to blame for the cheapness of the owner."

"How do you cope when it's crowded?"

"Sardonic humor."

"What do you get paid?"

"Not enough."

"What's playing tonight?"

"*Dressed to Kill*, just like it says on the marquee you were staring at a few minutes ago."

"Is it good?"

"Very good."

"Who's in it?"

"Angie Dickinson and Michael Caine, just like it says on the marquee you were staring at before you came in."

"Are you being sarcastic?"

"I'm being truthful and helpful."

"What's the movie about?"

"It's a thriller about how often a director can rip off other directors and repeat himself."

"I thought it was about some psycho-murdering shrink."

"See, you knew all along. I was just testing you."

"Are you going to start selling concessions soon?"

"Only if I have to."

"I'm hungry."

"Then I suggest you run down the street to the market, get some real food, and hurry back. You'll be cutting it close, but I think there's still time."

"But I want popcorn."

"Of course you do."

"With extra butter."

"Why?"

"Why?"

"Is there an echo in here?"

"Here he goes."

"Oh man."

"Yes."

"Because I like butter on my popcorn."

"Then again, I suggest you run down the street to the store and buy some real butter. There's still time if you hurry."

"Are you out of butter?"

"We have no butter here."

"But I can smell it."

"No. That isn't butter you smell. That's butter flavoring."

"Butter Flavoring, man!"

"So you do have butter."

"No, we have butter flavoring."

"That's what I want."

"Why?"

"Because I like it."

"Do you know what's in it?"

"Butter?"

"No. Not so much as a single drop."

"What's in it?"

"No one knows for sure. But there's rumors that float around the industry."

"Like what?"

"I don't think you want to know."

"Oh come on."

"Dude, I want to know."

"Me too."

"So do I."

"I'm telling you, it's not pleasant."

"Okay, enough of this. I'll bite. What's in it?"

"You're certain?"

"Yes."

"Is everyone here sure?"

"YES."

"One hundred percent?"

"You're scaring me a little."

"You should be scared."

"Don't scare her."

"Sir, I'm just getting you ready for the movie. Remember, it's a thriller. This is all part of the authentic theater experience. Cable can't give you this."

"So you don't really know what's in the butter?"

"Not butter."

"All right. Enough. What's in it?"

"Fess up, dude."

"Well, no one really knows for sure, but . . ."

"See, you don't know. It could be butter."

"BUT, I was saying before you interrupted me, and like I said earlier, there are rumors inside the industry."

"What industry? The vendor industry?"

"Sir, that was rude. There is no cause for demeaning a man at his station."

"That was harsh, man."

"Okay, all right, I'm sorry. What industry?"

"The entertainment industry."

"You're an insider, huh."

"Is that a question?"

"I don't know how much more of this I can take."

"At most, five to ten minutes. That's when I start the film."

"How do you keep your job?"

"By efficiently accomplishing all my tasks and chores with absolutely no supervision."

"But you're so obnoxious."

"Sir, at no time have I been anything other than responsive and hopefully helpful. If there has been any rudeness, it has not come from this side of the counter."

"That's the straight up truth, man."

"Okay, could you please tell me, all of us, what's in the butter?"

"We need the word on the butter, bro'."

"It's not butter."

"Okay, we understand, but how is it made?"

"You sure you want to know?"

"We paid for the tickets. We want to know."

"Everyone here feels the same way?"

"YES."

"Maybe I should close the box office first. I wouldn't want anyone walking in during the middle of this. I hate repeating myself. And it looks like we're sold out."

"For the love of Christ, would you please tell us?"

"Excuse me for saying so, sir, but that last question did not sound like you are filled with the love of Christ."

"I want the name of your manager."

"Bob."

"Bob what?"

"I don't know. He's just Bob to me."

"I want to talk with Bob."

"Well, you can leave a message with me, or you can try to reach him on a weekday here at the theater."

"I'm going to do that."

"Excellent."

"Okay, now can you please tell us?"

"I presume you mean the previously almost discussed ingredients, and manufacturing methods, for the elusive and allegedly addictive butter flavoring?"

"It's not addictive."

"I didn't say it was."

"Yes you did."

"I did not. I said allegedly addictive."

"It is not addictive. It's not like cigarettes."

"I don't know. Look how badly you want it."

"I am not addicted to butter flavoring."

"I'm glad. I don't want to be an enabler."

"Where did you hear it's addictive?"

"Well, when one works in the industry, one hears things."

"I can't take much more of this."

"Luckily, you don't have to. The movie is about to start."

"I don't know why anyone comes to this theater."

"And yet, amazingly, let me see now, from the second week of November 1980 to this very day in April 1981, yes, for the 22nd consecutive week, the 7:00 p.m. Saturday night show is a sellout."

"Does anyone else here have a problem with this guy?"

"Not really."

"What? You like this?"

"Sir, I come here almost every week."

"Me too."

"Yeah, I bring my friends."

"A lot of us do, man. I've seen that guy over there before."

"Why?"

"Most times, he's better than the movie."

"Yeah man, I thought we were gonna find out this week."

"Dude, I so thought we were gonna find out."

"I still want to know."

"Find out what?"

"The butter, man."

"Maybe the 9:30 show will get him."

"Yeah maybe, dude."

"It's showtime folks. You need to take your seats."

"I don't get it. You haven't sold any concessions."

"Not yet, anyway."

"I just don't get it."

"Don't worry, sir. You will. It's a thriller. I might even sneak another peek during the shower scene."

"I heard about that scene."

"It's a scorcher."

"Let's get a good seat."

"See you after the show."

"Will you tell us then?"

"Tell you what?"

"About the butter."

"All together now . . ."

"IT'S NOT BUTTER."

"He's funny."

Roger's Place

We were approaching Roger's door on 22nd Street just off Church in Noe Valley at 8:45 p.m., fifteen minutes after we were told to arrive.

"I hate being late," I said.

"Oh God, don't start," Cynthia admonished with slight irritation before adding, "It's only fifteen minutes. We haven't missed anything. I swear, you're so anal."

"Thanks, honey."

"Don't mention it. Now be a good boy and cheer up. We're going to have fun."

"If you say so."

"And if you're a really good boy, we'll have a lot of fun."

"Yeah? Well, don't make promises you don't intend to keep."

Cynthia grabbed me and kissed me like I had not been kissed since we started sleeping together six months to the day earlier.

She huskily advised, "Anniversaries aren't for promises, they're for surprises."

I smiled and said, "I'll drink sodas to that."

"You're such a responsible boy," Cynthia praised and all traces of lust were gone.

"That's me," I agreed, though the role of responsible one was already getting a little old.

"Are you okay, Dave?" Cynthia inquired just to be sure as we got to Roger's door.

"I hope so," I answered truthfully.

It wasn't the response she wanted, but before she could pursue it I knocked loudly, and almost instantly we heard Terry yelling, "Oh God, I hope it's them. They're so late."

I smugly smiled at Cynthia and for the first time since I'd begun dressing earlier, I felt hope for the evening. I really did like Roger and Terry. They worked with Cynthia at a Wharf restaurant and they treated me like a prince whenever I ate there.

Roger greeted each of us with a warm hug. I handed him a bottle of Chardonnay and he whisked it to the kitchen for chilling. In the living room were Big Tim, a black man who was born with the name Carlton, Little Tim, Terry, Hilary, who used to be Stan, and Roger's roommate, Joseph, a short, wiry Hispanic who had been Anita for a while.

"Goodie-goodie," Terry proclaimed as he rushed toward us. "The straights are here. I told you we'd get Dave to come."

"I bet I could make him come, too," proclaimed Hilary with his sultry voice, as he grabbed my arm and pulled me into the love seat next to him.

Cynthia roared with the laugh that was so distinctly hers. It was the kind of cackle that probably would have earned her a burning at the stake about 300 years ago. She easily broke her embrace with diminutive Terry and boldly sat on Little Tim's lap while absolutely planting him with a kiss.

Little Tim responded briefly, then broke the embrace and gasped, "Careful honey, you're going to ruin my reputation."

"Your reputation?" Terry roared. "Everyone here knows you're a closet dyke."

"Jesus Christ, Terry," Little Tim defended himself. "That's what I get for telling you anything."

"What's this?" Roger asked as he returned to the room. Little Tim was Roger's partner.

"Now look what you did," Little Tim accused Terry as the entire room exploded with laughter.

Roger let the roar die down before pursuing. "Terry, did you just say Little Tim was a dyke?"

Little Tim, a man so pretty that he would have made a stunning woman, deposited Cynthia on the couch, got up, and grabbed Roger's hand saying, "Roger sweetie, I meant to tell you this, but it just didn't seem to matter. And you know, it really doesn't matter."

Roger smiled like a man holding all the cards, and asked, "What doesn't matter?"

Little Tim stuck out his tongue at Terry before looking sheepishly at Roger and saying, "A long time ago, when I was just a boy in my old life, I had a girlfriend."

Roger rolled his eyes and proclaimed, "Oh God, is that all? I used to fuck women. I fucked lots of them."

A small amount of shock and revulsion reverberated around the room.

"You did?" asked Big Tim.

"You whore," announced Joseph.

"You slut," condemned Hilary.

"I knew there was a reason I liked you," I said.

"Oh shut up!" Terry yelled at me.

But Little Tim was thrilled. "Oh my hero, you did too? I'm so happy," and they embraced.

Roger patted Little Tim on the back and said, "But we're both past that now, right?"

"Oh God yes," Little Tim agreed and added, "I never liked it anyway. She was way too soft."

Their embrace broke and Roger shrugged. "I liked them."

"You are such a slut," admonished Big Tim, who looked like he was once a formidable athlete and probably still a bodybuilder.

Roger insisted, "I liked them. I just didn't love them," and he stroked Little Tim's cheek.

A chorus of aaahhhs followed from around the room.

But Terry wanted to know, "What could you have possibly liked about them?" Then he looked at Cynthia and added, "No disrespect to you, sweetie."

"None taken," Cynthia assured him while looking like she was having the time of her life.

Roger admitted, "Well, I didn't like the young ones. They didn't know what they were doing, at least not with me. But the older ones I liked a lot. I don't know, they were so . . ." and he paused, looking for just the right word.

"Hungry," I said.

"Yes, that's it," Roger agreed. "It was like they'd do anything to get fed."

I nodded.

When that laughter finally subsided, Terry asked Cynthia, "So which one are you, a younger one or an older one?"

Cynthia gracefully responded, "I'm definitely a younger one, unless I like what I'm being fed, then I'm a lot older."

There were oooohhs and aaaahhhs and then Hilary asked me, "So which is she with you, older or younger?"

"Older, younger, what's the difference to me? I'm a guy. I'm gonna get fed no matter what."

Amid the screaming, Hilary climbed on my lap and said, "You were so right, Roger. I like this one. You want to feed me, baby?"

I let him stroke my hair while the laughter subsided slightly before responding, "No thank you, I've had enough fruit today."

While everyone else laughed, Terry jumped up and pulled Hilary from my lap and proclaimed, "Now you just leave this poor straight alone. He's Cynthia's, and you're mine, and I've got a surprise that even a slut like you won't be able to resist."

Before Terry could reveal his surprise, Hilary announced, "Well I've got a surprise for you, Terry Phillip, I'm on the rag."

The room shook from the noise, but above the din, Terry yelled, "Oh yeah? Well you can just hang your rag on this," and he unbuttoned his shirt to reveal a thin golden chain hanging from one nipple to the other.

"OH LOVER!" screamed Hilary, and then buried his head in Terry's chest.

"Take it easy, you bitch," Terry scolded and pushed Hilary to arm's length. "You just be good and stop picking on poor David. He can't help it if he's straight," and he winked at me before adding, "Though God knows, you are a mighty waste of talent."

"Dinner should be ready," announced Roger above the laughter. "Would one of you girls give me a hand?"

As we moved toward the dining room, Cynthia whispered to me, "How you doing now?"

I whispered back facetiously, "Scared. Very scared."

She smiled, squeezed my arm, wetly kissed my ear, and whispered, "I do love you, you know."

I knew Cynthia well enough by that point to realize this statement meant everything and nothing simultaneously. I wasn't going to be too swayed in any direction, so all I said was, "That's nice."

We took our seats and had a wondrous meal. There were sautéed asparagus tips, perfectly broiled portabella mushrooms stuffed with razor-thin slices of caramelized elephant garlic and parmesan, and an unbelievably delicious quiche made of Jarlsburg cheese, spinach, and Maui sweet onions. Everything was served on a bed of sautéed arugula and framed by heart-shaped, extra virgin deep-fried goat cheese polenta.

Dinner conversation was lively and the wine flowed freely for everyone but me.

Roger asked, "Not even a glass?"

"I don't drink and drive anymore. I had a bad accident and a real close call with the law once, and that was the end of that."

Terry said, "But honey, if you drink too much here, you can just spend the night. Everyone else is. You two are invited."

I looked around the table and noticed everyone else there except Cynthia had a mustache. I briefly thought of my old hairdresser friend, Toni. I said, "That's very kind, but no thank you. I really don't want to drink."

Big Tim commented, "My God, you are straight. Were you raised in Utah?"

This brought up the topic of religion and each of us told what faith, if any, that we'd been raised.

I told them that on my best days, I was agnostic, but most of the time, I was atheist.

Joseph asked, "So you don't believe in heaven?"

I replied, "Actually, I do believe in heaven, but it's not like anything we've been traditionally taught. I think the concept of heaven, or nirvana, or someplace that houses our souls after we die is nonsense and selfish. It's vanity. I think, when we die, the only place we live on is in the memories of those we leave behind. The quality of those memories is determined by our actions while we live. The good memories we leave are heaven and the bad memories are hell. So we better try to be good, not for our sake, but for those who survive us."

"I like that a lot," Roger said sincerely.

"I don't," Hilary insisted. "I want to go someplace that doesn't hate me for being gay."

"Aren't you there right now?" I asked.

"Oh, I really like that," Roger stated and everyone agreed.

Another strong reaction came after Cynthia proudly identified herself as a member of a group called PRENARIUS.

Joseph winced and said, "Ave Maria, what could that be? It even sounds hideous."

Cynthia was not the least bit swayed by their ignorance or skepticism. She explained that PRENARIUS was an organization based on sound scientific principle and the staunch belief in reincarnation. She said we're all just souls living our lives over and over again as we try to work out the bullshit from our past and move on to our higher selves.

Terry declared, "Oooooo, that sounds kind of trendy. Who got you into it?"

Cynthia admitted, "My parents."

Little Tim said, "God, and I thought my parents were weird for being Christian Scientists."

"At least they aren't EST heads," commented Hilary.

"Don't you mean EST holes?" corrected Roger. "They're the worst."

There was agreement with this around the table and that was as far as Cynthia was made to explain her spiritual choice. I wished it had gone on a little longer, because I sensed I was not the only one at Roger's that felt PRENARIUS sounded like a wacky cult. I hoped the skepticism of Cynthia's other friends might give her pause. But that did not happen and I knew it was going to take something far greater to shake Cynthia from her belief. I'd given it close to my best shot. But if anyone else at that table considered pursuing the topic, they let it go for the evening, because a serious conversation would certainly have meant an end to the fun for the night.

As the subject changed and discussion continued, I kept glancing across the table at Cynthia, who was utterly within her element. Men who she could fearlessly flirt with surrounded her. With them, she could be one of the guys. She was at the height of her masculinity and they were at the depths of theirs. I was more attracted to her at that moment than I had been since we met.

Dinner was followed by an impromptu fashion show, with some of the boys trying on Joseph's wigs for all occasions. Cynthia was right there with them, suggesting jewelry and other accessories. I stayed in the living room and applauded the parade along with Roger and Terry. Every time Hilary came in, he would either sachet over and slither into my lap or go directly to Terry and unbutton his shirt. He would then examine Terry's chest, or give the brand new chain some teasing tugs.

The novelty of men in wigs soon wore thin and Roger suggested we go dancing.

"I dance with David first," announced Hilary.

Roger noticed my slightly uncomfortable smile, put his arm around my shoulder, and whispered, "David, does your mother know what you're doing tonight?"

I relaxed, giggled, and gave Roger a warm hug. I like him the most. He is my height, about ten years older and his hair is thinning in the same manner I was told to expect from mine. He is doing nothing to hide this and that makes me like him even more. I told him that ironically enough, I had spoken with my mother earlier and the last thing I said to her was that I was going out with the boys that night.

To further calm me, Roger insisted we do our dancing at The Stud because it was only about 90 percent gay. I thanked him for his consideration and advised facetiously that even one percent more would have been a deal breaker.

I certainly danced with energy and enthusiasm, though dancing has never been my forte. I bumped and grinded with all the men in our party and nimbly avoided, as best I could, the men I did not know. It might have been my paranoia, but some of them seemed to view me as fresh chum. I showed my best moves getting off the dance floor as soon as I heard the start of "Tonight's the Night" by Rod Stewart.

As I nimbly retreated, Terry yelled, "You chicken."

I smiled, nodded, and kept moving until I saw Cynthia standing by the bar watching me. There was sweat glistening on her neck and her satin blouse was unbuttoned below her low-cut bra, revealing the perfectly shaped cleavage I so admired.

I approached asking, "You having a good time?"

"Hell yes. How about you, baby?"

I looked around the room before answering, "I'm having a great time. These are just some good old boys."

She suddenly pressed herself fully against me, wrapping one arm around my waist while her other hand grabbed my ass.

I gasped, "Damn honey, happy anniversary. I sure hope you're like this later when we're alone."

She looked at me lustily and asked, "You want to be alone right now, Dave?"

I briefly looked around the room and said, "Cyn, you pick the damnedest time."

Cynthia grabbed my hand and led me around the bar. She boldly pulled me into a dimly lit restroom, where we found a line of men standing side by side at the long urinal trough. Almost in unison, they turned and stared at us. We did an abrupt about-face and Cynthia plowed a path through the crowd at the door. She pressed against me while marching us at a brisk pace, through fog and one red light, down the street to where I'd parked her car. She reached into my pocket for the keys and found everything she wanted. Before unlocking the back door, she put her lips within an inch of mine and said, "I told you anniversaries are for surprises. Right now, I'm surprisingly hungry, and I want to be fed."

The gnawing silence of late at night in the city
A car
A siren
A person
Two people
How quaint

But even when there is nothing
There is always
The far off wailing
Of the low drone

December 1981

Mothers

I woke up one fine May morning in 1982 with a pain in my neck. *I must have slept on it wrong*, I thought, and then proceeded to forget about it, except when I turned my head to the left. This went on for days and while I realized it could not have happened while I slept, I still did not pay much attention to what I presumed was some sort of muscle strain. But after a week, I noticed I was taking aspirin on a daily basis, about three times a day, and the discomfort was becoming persistent. This went on for five more days.

That's when I saw the lump. It was halfway down my neck, midway between my right ear and chin. I have no idea how I didn't notice it before. But one morning, I looked in the mirror, turned my head to the left and there it was, about half the size of a golf ball. It was not acutely tender to the touch, but the area around it was sore, and there was the beginning of restriction in movement.

I showed it to my roommate and his initial comment, "Nice boil," was funny, though not very helpful.

When Roger saw it, however, he wanted to take me to his doctor immediately. I couldn't, but I promised him I'd go to the school infirmary and see the nurse and whoever was on call the next day. When Cynthia saw it that night, she lost her appetite.

I was with the nurse for approximately ninety seconds. She took one look at my neck and told me not to move. She returned with Dr. Garza, the physician on campus that day. He looked at my neck and asked me a rather chilling question. "Does anyone in your family, that you know of, have lymphatic cancer, or any other form of cancer?"

I only knew that some in the family tree had passed from the big C, but, specifically, I did not know exactly who or what kind. Dr. Garza told me he would like me to stay right there while he called a couple of specialists in the city to see which one could see me first.

That was enough for me. I said that wouldn't be necessary, but I would appreciate if I could use his phone to call home.

That was yesterday a little after noon. I was on the 7:00 PSA flight to LAX last night and in the office of my old family physician at 9:00 this morning. Following a brief exam, I was told to take the elevator to the 10th floor to see a specialist who was waiting for me.

That is where I am right now. I am in the waiting room of a surgeon, Dr. Windsor. It is the first time in my life I've ever been truly afraid. I am legitimately scared.

At least I convinced Mom to let me come by myself. She is freaking out and probably contributing to my level of stress. Granted, I understand why she's concerned. I'm her only child. But I cannot deal with her anxiety and my own rising level of panic at the same time. It is already a difficult dynamic, but if surgery is needed, and my family doctor saw no way around that, recovery at home would be problematic, if not counterproductive to healing.

Try to relax. I don't know what I'm dealing with yet. I don't want to make it worse by getting my boxers in a bunch about Mom.

I felt a momentary surge of creature comfort when I spotted a *Highlights* magazine in the rack next to the reception window. I suddenly have a deep need for pajamas and cinnamon toast. I'm feeling achy. I think I have a fever.

The timing of this lump could not be worse. Our final project presentation is next Tuesday in Group Discussion and we're supposed to be rehearsing every day between now and then. We even planned to spend Saturday and Sunday at Jessica's flat working nonstop, with a full dress rehearsal Sunday night for a few friends and, hopefully, some members of the San Francisco Arts and Athletics organization. They are the group planning the 1st Gay Olympic Games for later this year.

I'm so excited about our presentation. I wrote the entire thing, but everyone in the group contributed hugely to the research. I will never forget the day Tim Yu introduced the idea of a mock debate, or panel discussion on the Gay Olympics. When he brought it up, my initial reaction was not exactly enthusiastic. I'd heard about the Gay Olympics briefly from Roger because he knew some people that wanted to participate, including Big Tim, but I did not know any details, and I had no idea how potentially cool the event could be. But everyone else became excited. I suppose having almost half the group comprised of gay people contributed to the exhilaration, but no one was expecting Tim to tip the lifestyle scales by coming out then and there. The emotion he showed, and how long it had been inside him wanting to be revealed, was real and powerful. Plus, I know he also hopes to compete in the Games. It might be the fever, but I get goose bumps just thinking about it. We didn't understand Tim at first, because his voice is soft and his face was toward the floor. But when Jessica asked him to look up and speak louder, we saw the tears. We asked him what was the matter. All he said was, "I am gay. I have always been gay. I will always be gay. There. I said it."

Cynthia started crying, followed quickly by Carl, Jessica, Connie, Sherrice, and then me. One of the student teachers for Speech 551 wanted to know if we were okay. We told him, and he got weepy. Several members of other groups joined in. I've never experienced a moment like that before. It was beautiful and inspiring.

From there, the idea evolved quickly and efficiently. Everyone had research to do, in addition to developing the persona they were going to portray in the presentation/debate. That's been fun. We've even started calling each other by our presentation names outside class. Connie hates the last name I've chosen for her, but the rest of the group out voted her. She half jokingly said she'd like to kick me in the balls for it, but if she did, I would then be completely, and not just mostly, worthless to Cynthia. I also told the group if I could live my entire life with the last name Morehead, they could live an hour of their lives with the names I gave them. I've taken to being my character, the Reverend David Straight, in all sorts of situations. I've been driving my roommate a little crazy. Joseph contributed wigs for every group member. Some of those rugs transform us into different people. The skullcap with the bad comb-over he found for Carl makes him look like he's in his fifties. Plus, Carl's Howard Cosell impersonation made his character, and the writing of the entire presentation, come alive.

My current predicament has happened so fast; Cynthia has to tell everyone in the group later today. They have to continue rehearsing without me and we'll just see how things develop. I also left a message for our professor, Dr. Randle, and Cynthia will explain everything to him. Hopefully, if I'm delayed down here, we can get a later date for the presentation. All the dates are taken, but maybe we can switch with another group. I don't know. It's out of my hands right now.

I'm back at my parents' house. I met with the surgeon, Dr. Windsor, and sure enough, the lump has got to go. But the good news is that I convinced him to do it tomorrow as an outpatient. I'll have the surgery at 10:00 in the morning, be out of the hospital by early afternoon, and catch the 8:00 flight to San Francisco tomorrow night. Thankfully, Dr. Windsor doesn't think the operation will be very complicated. Because he'll only use local anesthetic, I won't be knocked out, so they will not have to keep me overnight. Of course, that also means I'll be awake for the entire procedure.

You know, that's pretty fucking weird. I'm only now completely realizing the deal I made. I'm going to be lying there, wide awake, as a guy cuts my neck open about three inches from my right ear. Then he's going inside my neck to extract a growth that he thinks is starting to twist around other tissue.

He would not speculate what it could be, but it needs to come out and be analyzed. It will take a laboratory a few days to determine exactly what it is, and whether it's malignant or benign.

I have to wait before I find out. This sucks.

But at least I won't be home. Let Mom freak out on her own—and make no mistake, she is freaking.

Her condition was made rather comically worse by the phone call she got from my group this afternoon. I hadn't come home yet from the doctor. I was walking along the beach, trying to get everything clear in my head before facing Mom. Anyway, they called from Dr. Randle's office on a speakerphone and Mom didn't know, as she put it, who or what she was speaking to.

I wish I could have been present for that talk. My mom was on the phone with Connie? Are you kidding me? I can't wait to hear about it from Cynthia.

By the way, Mom thought Cynthia sounded very nice, though perhaps a little bossy. She also said that based on the conversation, it was hard for her to know when she was listening to women or men. She said some of the women sounded like men and vice versa. I told her that I'd be sure to pass that on to the group and she was horrified.

But then, she was generally horrified at everything I said after I got home. She couldn't understand how the doctor can do this with me as an outpatient. She thinks I should be kept in the hospital until they find out what is wrong. Then, if it's cancer, they should just start the treatment immediately. I also think she's hurt that I'm leaving so soon. It's been almost a year since I was home for an extended stay and there's nothing like an illness to reignite the maternal instinct. Dad only says the doctor knows what he's doing and that I need to get back to school, and thank goodness for Dad. I'm so glad he's retired and home more.

But neither of them understands why I insist on going out tonight. They think I should stay home, and go to bed early. They are probably right. I have to be at the hospital at 8:00 in the morning. But there's no fucking way. I'm getting my neck sliced open in about seventeen hours and I'm going to hear every moment. That is not something I ever expected happening to me. In fact, I don't know anyone it's happened to. Certainly, Raves and Rod had never heard of it when I called them. In fact, it sounded like a pretty damn good reason for all of us to get together.

Okay, it's later now, much later. 4:00 a.m. later. Should be asleep. Been drinking a little. More than a little. Started with Guinness on tap at McGinty's Pub. Had a few. Excellent stuff. Ended with a jug of Gallo red I got from Vons market. Horrid. My tongue is stained. I'm going to feel real good when the alarm goes off after a consummately refreshing 180 minutes or less of sleep. But I'm so excited. Raves gave me a little portable tape recorder with a built-in stereo condenser microphone and a brand new 120-minute cassette. Gonna try to bootleg the surgery. Don't know if I can, but I'm gonna try. Had a great time with the boys. Cranked the shit out of *Delta Four* by Synergy in Dad's car with all the windows down and the sound blaring around the reverb heavy, completely concrete-enclosed basement garage of Rod's apartment building. We were lucky someone didn't call the cops. I was also reminded why I don't like to drink and drive. I'm damn lucky I didn't get pulled over on the way home. Fuck, I think the hangover is already starting.

I am now aboard PSA flight #72 to San Francisco. I have a large bandage on my neck and enough pain pills to keep me sedate and silly for the next few days. I was told not to mix the pain medicine with alcohol. Right. Just as soon as we're airborne, I want the strongest fucking drink they've got aboard this cattle car.

Perhaps it was the nervous adrenaline, but I barely felt any aftereffects of drinking when Mom awakened me this morning. I was tired, because I had not slept much, but no hangover to speak of. I showered, brushed my teeth, marinated my gums and tongue with mouthwash for five minutes, and was out the door with the folks. Once in St. John's Hospital, I was told to undress and get into the ever popular ass cheeks visible gown. I have no idea why I was forced to wear that flimsy, pathetic piece of single-ply tissue. Further, why did I have to go sans underwear? At least I don't have a hairy crack. The hospital gown was also the end of any chance to use the recording device.

I was wheeled into the operating room, placed on the table, and instructed to turn my head as far as I could comfortably turn to my left. A pillow was slid under the left side of my face and I was told to try and remain as motionless as possible. A small towel was draped over the top part of my face and head, completely covering my eyes. They began administering Novocain to my neck. I was assured the only pain I would feel was the sting of the initial shot. I told them I hoped that was true. Then they told me not to speak anymore, unless I felt pain at any point during the procedure.

I said, "But you just said the only pain I'm going to feel is the first shot."

I was reminded to not speak, but that I had nothing to worry about regarding pain. The anesthesiologist said, "Your neck is going to be so numb, you might wonder if there is anything between your scalp and shoulders."

I replied, "And not for the first time."

More shots were given and I was asked whether I felt any pressure or pain as they pushed my neck. Eventually, I could not feel when they touched me, but I could always feel when they pressed on my neck, because it felt like I was being choked. They said this was normal and that I should breathe through my nose.

I heard people in the room, shoes squeaking on the floor, and the occasional clinking of metallic devices fairly close to my head. Then from above and slightly to my left came a new voice saying, "David, my name is Simone. I'm a nurse and I'll be here to assist you. The procedure will begin shortly."

Oh my god, what a voice. It was soft, warm, and completely British. She sounded like that hot chick in *Logan's Run*. What was her name? Yes. She sounded like Jenny Agutter. And that meant if she sounded like Jenny Agutter, there was a reasonable presumption she would look something like Jenny Agutter.

I had to be careful. That kind of thought was dangerous when wearing only a single-ply gown and a blanket not much thicker.

In fact, I needed to be really, really careful.

I was suddenly utterly failing in my efforts to be careful. I needed to think of something fast, something to distract me. THINK. Concentrate.

Butter flavoring. Yes, butter flavoring. There you go. Down you go. Retreat. Yes. Thank you, butter flavoring. I never thought I would find a reason to be grateful for that wretched sludge.

Keep that thought. Hold on to it. Because when she talks, the butter starts to melt, oh yeah, and the popcorn starts to pop. Jenny baby . . . BUTTER FLAVORING.

So I was thrillingly uncomfortable for the start of the operation, but at least I was distracted.

Dr. Windsor came in and said, "Good morning, David. I'm sure you've already been told to move as little as possible, and during the procedure I only want you to speak if you feel any pain or sensation of cold or hot. Do you understand?"

"Yes."

"Are you comfortable?"

"Yes."

"Simone is the nurse attending you. Have you been introduced?"

"Oh yeah."

Dr. Windsor continued, "She will have one of her hands close to your left hand at all times. If you need to say something, touch her and she'll let me know. A little discomfort or pressure is normal and we'll give you something to help with that. Of course, if you feel any sharp pain or temperature sensation, let me know immediately. I cannot stress enough, however, the importance of staying still and quiet. Do you understand?"

"Yes."

"Are you comfortable?"

"Slice away, doc."

"Pardon me?"

"I said, slice away, doc."

"That's what I thought you said. Mr. Morehead, at this point you should cease any attempts at levity. I enjoyed our conversation in the office yesterday, but any humor right now could be detrimental to the success of the procedure. Do you understand?"

I was reminded that the day before, Dr. Windsor struck me as extremely meticulous and somewhat anal, like someone who brushes the teeth of their pets. In my nervousness, I worked hard to make him smile. I imagined how he would sound, little brush in hand saying, "Here kitty-kitty." But he was correct in reminding me this was a time for business.

I answered, "Yes sir."

"Excellent. Nurse?"

Simone touched my arm and then placed a rubber ball into my left hand. She said, "If you need to, squeeze this ball. Sometimes this helps if you feel a little discomfort. Anything more than a little discomfort and you touch me, all right?"

"Okay," I said while thinking, *But if I drop the ball, may I squeeze your thigh?*

Dr Windsor asked, "Are we all ready?"

I thought, *Wait a minute. A ball is what you're giving me? When you said you're giving me something to help with discomfort, you were referring to this rubber ball? This handball?*

Simone asked, "David, are you okay?"

I rubbed my ball hand up and down on her gloved hand.

Simone said, "That's good, David. Up and down means yes, and sideways will mean no. All right?"

I kept rubbing up and down.

Simone said, "You can stop now, David."

Butter flavoring, butter flavoring.

Dr. Windsor asked, "Are we ready to proceed?"

Simone said, "Yes."

The procedure began and I didn't have to think of butter flavoring again. It was only a few minutes before I started to feel discomfort and I commenced working the ball. It was shortly thereafter when I felt unmistakable pain.

I touched Simone and then Dr. Windsor said, "David, we're going to give you more Novocain now."

They did and proceeded for a while longer without incident.

Then another voice, a female voice asked, "Doctor, do you see where it goes?"

Dr. Windsor replied, "Yes."

A few moments later, Dr. Windsor said, "David, we're going to give you more Novocain, because we're having to go a little deeper than we originally thought."

I felt nothing, but something about the way the doctor spoke caused me to tense.

Simone began rubbing my arm and said, "Everything is fine, David. Nothing out of the ordinary."

I rubbed her hand in gratitude.

Dr. Windsor said, "We're going to resume now."

That's when things started getting weird. When the doctor dug into my neck, for the first time I could feel matter being moved around, and not just the lump. The sensation of choking and tugging was much stronger. Then I felt something cold followed immediately by sharp pain.

I squeezed that hard rubber ball almost flat and reached for Simone.

She immediately said, "Doctor?"

He withdrew from my neck and said, "Yes, Dave?"

"I felt cold and also like things are getting pinched in there. Then, I felt real pain."

There was a pause and then Dr. Windsor said, "David, here is the situation. The lump is not the issue right now. The problem is that it has grown arms that have wrapped around other tissue. We need to extract those arms in addition to the lump. That is also why you are feeling choking sensations. The arms are clinging tight and actually clamping down on tissue closer to your throat. In order to extract everything, I'm having to go deeper than the Novocain can reach."

"Can you give me more Novocain?" I asked.

He sighed and Simone put her hand on my arm. Then Dr. Windsor continued, "Mr. Morehead, we have a choice to make right now. The first choice is that we completely anesthetize you, we finish the procedure, you won't feel a thing, and you'll spend at least one night or more in the hospital. The other choice is that we proceed right now, but you need to know I cannot give you any more Novocain. I don't think I'm going to have to dig past where you have been numbed. You may feel something touching you past the numbness, but no more cutting. If I'm incorrect, we'll both know and then we'll knock you out. However, I believe I can extract everything pretty quickly at this point. I see where it's going. But in order to get there, and not cause you substantial pain, I'm going to have to move things around a little. I don't think it's going to hurt, but it will feel unusual."

I asked, "What do you mean by unusual?"

Dr. Windsor said, "You will feel things being moved around that ordinarily would not be moved."

I asked, "How long will it take?"

Dr. Windsor answered, "Just a few minutes."

This time I sighed and then said, "Go for it, but if you have to dig at all past the numbing, please stop. You can knock me out and do your worst."

Dr. Windsor asked, "So you want us to go ahead right now?"

"Yes."

Simone said, "You're very brave."

I said, "You've got the sexiest voice I've ever heard."

There was a pause and then Dr. Windsor asked, "David, are you ready for us to proceed?"

"Yes."

Well friends, it's like this . . . the remainder of my procedure took about five minutes. There was a brief moment of pain, though not long enough to make me call for the knock-out punch. But the doctor was correct in warning me about how it would feel.

You see, when the doctor started moving things around a little, what he meant was that he was going to have to move things out of the way in order to adequately find a spot to grab and extract the entire octopus of foreign matter out of my throat, neck, and incision. When he did this, I experienced the strangest single moment of my life to date. From the top and back of my head, I suddenly felt all the skin being pulled forward, down, and heading for the hole in my neck. My complete scalp was moved toward my face, and my face was shifted into my neck. The entirety of it was being pulled . . . thataway. I understood what an autopsy would feel like.

Then they were done. They stitched me up and told me to stay still and not attempt to get up until I was instructed to do so.

I asked, "Simone, Doctor, someone . . . is everything on my face going to be where it was before?"

They laughed. Dr. Windsor said, "Yes, Dave, everything is exactly where it was, but I understand why you feel that way. Try to remain still and relax for now. Simone will stay with you."

A side note here from my seat on flight #72 . . . it may not be smart to mix alcohol with whatever the hell they gave me for pain, but for the record, I am feeling no discomfort whatsoever right now. In fact, I'm kind of frisky. The curvaceous blonde in the tight knit dress to my immediate right in the window seat is aiding this coltish sensation. Due to the intimate proximity, she might have been reading what I'm writing. She might be reading right now.

So if you are, know that I would like to wrap you as best I can in gauze, parade you through the Castro on Halloween night, and then probe for weaknesses in the fabric while standing under a showerhead.

It is many hours later now. Two thirty-seven Saturday morning, to be precise. I am back at my apartment, having been dropped off here by Cynthia a little while ago. I was going to spend the night at her place, but, unfortunately, we had a little misunderstanding that did not end well.

It certainly started well. I had an erection the entire drive home and I chose to let it air out and roam around a bit while I stared at Cynthia from the passenger seat. She was shocked, distracted, and then utterly turned on by the time we reached her flat. All I had to do was lay back and enjoy the ride. Unfortunately, in her haste to have at me, she flung my backpack to the other side of the room and many of the contents spilled. Sometime later, while I contentedly napped, she grabbed my journal and read the latest entry.

Of course, I have asked that she not read my journal and to the best of my knowledge, until this very night, she respected this request. If I had been awake, we would have talked and I would have told her about flirting with Simone. I probably would have told her about the woman on the plane and how, in my drugged and altered mind, I got turned on. That would have explained my behavior on the drive home. I probably would not have told her how the woman, an attorney named Debbie in her mid-thirties I'd guess, handed me her card as we were getting up to leave, told me to give her a call, and said that she preferred fishnet over gauze.

But at least it would have been explained and probably understood, given the stressful nature of the situation.

Without context, to Cynthia it simply read like I'm some renegade rogue male, relentlessly pursuing any available port to dock my dinghy. I tried to explain that Simone did not look like Jenny Agutter. She was in her fifties at least and a grandmother. She said my comment about her voice was the nicest thing anyone other than her husband of thirty-two years had said to her since she was a teen.

But Cynthia did not want to hear that. She acknowledged she should not have read the journal, but, once she did, the damage was done. In truth, we have been arguing more and having sex less. Her bogus religion is the cause, but she did not want to talk about that tonight. She had the goods on me and she took the offensive. The entire matter struck me as unfair, so I was less than supportive of her. Finally, after about an hour of bickering and evading the real issues, she grabbed her keys and said she was taking me home. I was both relieved and pissed.

I wish I'd stayed in Santa Monica with my parents for a while longer. That's a strange thing to admit, but it's true. Mom was pretty mellow after the surgery. She was different as well. It almost seemed like she was relieved that I was leaving, but I cannot be certain of that, especially given my drug-induced frame of mind. What I do know is that she had a gift for me that was really cool. Over dinner the night before, I told my parents about the group presentation. While I was in surgery, she went to a party and costume shop and purchased a priest's smock. It will mostly cover the bandage and was the one thing missing to make my character complete. I was moved when she gave it to me and somewhat regretful that I was leaving so soon. I hugged her extra long at the airport. I hope she knows I love her. Dad shook my hand and told me he was proud of me going into that operating room with my eyes open and taking it like a man. That made me giggle slightly and I hugged him hard as well.

Damn, I could be snug and cozy in my old bed, being served my favorite childhood meals, watching television and waiting for the test results. Instead, I'm sitting here at my desk, my neck has begun a low-level throb, the fridge is almost empty, the corner store is closed, my roommate is snoring, my girlfriend is pissed at me, and my group is anxiously awaiting my arrival to resume work later today.

There's something I didn't have time to write earlier. After the surgery, I was allowed to sit up, drink some juice, and eat several cookies. I met Simone and we chatted. She was a very nice woman and I hope she did not notice my excitement when we first met. I don't think she did, but then, she is a nurse and used to seeing all sorts of things. There was no weirdness between us. There was, however, one exceedingly weird moment. After about forty-five minutes or an hour, I felt well enough to leave. I was walking around the room and my vitals were fine. I drank orange juice, ate a muffin, and had a few more cookies. They took my blood pressure, checked my pulse, the doctor looked me over and Simone was going to retrieve my clothes.

Dr. Windsor told me that whatever the test results might show, it was a good thing we got the lump out, because it was threatening to choke me. He said that if I'd waited another ten days or so, the extraction would have probably involved removal of some voice-related tissue.

Just before Simone left, she asked, "Would you like to see it?"

I wasn't sure what she meant, so I asked, "See what?"

"The lump we removed."

"Don't they need it for testing?"

Dr. Windsor said, "They already have the sample they need. The rest of it is probably in the laboratory. She could bring it with your clothes."

Well why not, I thought and said, "Okay, just don't put it in my pocket."

While she was gone, I considered my decision. It was kind of strange. I was about to look at a lump taken from inside my body that could eventually lead to my demise. I started feeling a little light-headed.

She returned with my clothes in one hand and a glass cup in the other. Before handing me the clothes, she extended the glass and said, "Here it is."

It was the size of a very large marble. It was pink. It had arms.

I fainted on the spot.

It was another half hour before they let me go. I came to pretty quickly and told Simone to get that thing out of my sight. She was apologetic and I assured her she had not scarred me forever. I can only hope that is true. I don't want to write any more about the lump.

It is now late Saturday night as I write this. Cynthia showed up a couple of hours before dawn this morning in a miserable state. I was in bed, getting drowsy from another pain pill when I heard the soft knocking and also someone sniffling. She was a guilty mess. We didn't talk. I was too tired, so I just led her to bed. We slept entwined, something I ordinarily hate doing. I'm a big guy and I need space. Besides, having a woman's body pressed against mine usually leads to an unattended erection and that is extremely difficult to tolerate. But this time, it was different. Must have been the drugs.

We still didn't talk much when she got up. We both said we were sorry and that seemed to suffice for now. There is distance, however.

Within an hour of Cynthia leaving, I started receiving phone calls and then Roger arrived. I filled him in on everything that happened and he simply took over. He answered the phone; he monitored the length of time I spoke with people. He wanted me to rest, eat, rest, relax, drink lots of water, and take my Tylenol. He insisted I stop taking the heavy pain medicine. He said that stuff was horrible for me, that I was a big boy and could take a little pain. He gave complete updates to each group member when they called. Everyone agreed I needed one more day of rest before I resumed rehearsal for our presentation. There was one very interesting phone call from my mother. Roger answered and I could tell by his voice that Mom was concerned. Adeptly, Roger lied and told her that he was a nurse from college. When the infirmary heard I was back, Roger told her, he volunteered to come over and help me. He said I was one of the most popular and important students on campus and it was his pleasure to be of assistance. They chatted for several minutes and Roger seemed very interested in what she had to say. It was really sweet.

But the most intriguing part for me was that during the entire conversation, Roger did not sound the least bit gay. He used an unaffected voice for my mother. He sounded masculine and completely straight. He saw my open-mouthed reaction and turned his back. He told my mother I was napping and he promised to have me call her later. She told him I should call when I felt up to it and that she would be resting more easily now that she knew I was in such good hands.

"You faker," I accused when he hung up.

"I'm going to the store," he replied evasively, and with a lisp.

I laughed and said, "I want an explanation."

He grabbed his rucksack and headed toward the door. "If you don't start drinking that water I gave you, you're going to get an enema."

"Wouldn't that make you happy?" I mockingly asked.

"No, it would not," he insisted and was out the door.

Roger was gone long enough for me to fall asleep. I heard my roommate get up and complain that it was like Grand Central Station around there. I told him I was sorry and he said he was joking, but I couldn't be entirely certain. I think he was expecting to have the place to himself for a few days. I told him I'd be out of his hair all Sunday and most of Monday. That seemed to make him feel better, and he was genuinely concerned about my health. He showed me the movies he'd recorded from cable while I was gone and that was kind. He left fairly soon after getting up and I fell asleep again.

When I awakened, I smelled delicious food. There was a strong aroma of garlic. I got up and Roger had made chicken and vegetable soup, Caesar salad, and garlic bread. It all looked like something my mother would have made. It was certainly similar to what my mother would have cooked had I stayed home. I started to cry.

Roger said, "Oh baby, someone has to mother you today. Why don't you sit down and eat? I've got you all to myself and we can chat."

Again, there was barely a trace of lisp in his voice. He sounded like any straight man. I was as confused as I was moved.

Roger insisted, "Eat first, then we'll talk."

The food was so good. Roger was generally a no meat vegetarian, but he made an exception in this case, because the rotisserie bird he bought for the broth was simply too succulent.

The Caesar salad was very similar and perhaps even richer than the salad my mother made. But the star of the meal, and what truly touched me, was the garlic bread. It was made exactly like my mother made it, with generous bits of fresh oregano and topped with extra melted and browned Parmesan. We ate the entire loaf he broiled.

I was stuffed to the brim and grateful beyond words. I cleared the table and kissed Roger on the cheek on my way to the sink. He beamed and I insisted he stay in his seat while I did the dishes.

When I finished, I made a pot of tea and we sat in the only two chairs in the living room. I was ready to pepper him with questions, but Roger looked like he wanted to speak. I waited patiently while he gathered his thoughts.

Finally he looked at me and said, "Sometimes I get very tired of being a fag. I never get tired of the sex, mind you, or the freedom that comes with being gay. But I do tire of the stereotypical fag part. I think it holds me back. I think it holds us all back. It makes us a joke, a cliché, something other than what we are, which is human beings like everyone else and specifically for me, a man."

I commented, "But you're bisexual, right? Or you were at one point."

He shook his head. "Not really. I've always been gay. I fucked women because my dick was constantly hard and there were no gay men around that attracted me. Where I grew up, a small town in Ohio, you had to really look hard to find someone, and you ran the risk of getting stomped. I knew early on that I was more attracted to men than women, but it would ensure my survival until I could leave that place to keep my true feelings hidden and learn how to fuck with what was available while I waited."

Despite the serious nature of what he said, I burst into laughter. I said, "Jesus Roger, I know women that would kick your ass if they heard you talk like that."

He nodded in acknowledgment, but added, "Like you haven't done the same thing?"

"Granted," I admitted and then continued, "But then, why the lisp? When did that start?"

Roger said, "As soon as I got here. I mean, the very first day I walked into the Castro, I was a complete lispy swish."

"Why? Was it necessary to meet people?"

Roger considered the question and said, "I suppose it's like going to a foreign country. It helps if you speak the language."

"But you're trapped by it now."

He said, "Not all the time, and not as much as when I first got here. When Tim and I are by ourselves, we often drop the lisp and sound like any other guys, though we are both neater than most men, including gays."

"I noticed that."

Roger raised an eyebrow and said, "Yes, and I've noticed that you have improved quite a bit in that regard since we met."

"There you have it," I gleefully admitted. "The gay influence."

Roger furrowed his brows at me and said, "You know Dave, and Tim agrees with me on this, a different chromosome or two in you and you'd be gay."

I smiled, not because I agreed, but because I'd come a long way to hear something like that and not react badly. I said, "Well, you and Tim can speculate all you want about my chromosomes, but there is nothing homosexual or bisexual about me. I could neither suck cock nor have one inserted in my ass. Ever. No."

Roger instructed, "You don't know what you're missing."

I insisted, "And I don't want to know."

Roger pursued, "Aren't you even a little curious about it?"

"No," I was adamant. "Roger, I'm not even into anal sex with women. I tried it once, but stopped immediately because I thought she was going to split in half."

Roger nodded. "Yeah, I know, but men are built differently than women. The sensation is completely different for us."

"Whatever, Roger, why are you pursuing this with me? I'm not interested."

Roger scolded, "You should be. We've become friends, right? Don't you talk about sex with your friends?"

"Of course I do, though I write about it more than I talk about it. But that's just me."

Roger nodded. "Sure, that's what is normal for you. Did you ever consider the same things are normal for us?"

"I haven't really thought about it," I admitted.

"Well, David, here's the deal. If you want to be my friend, it can't just be with the part of me that you relate to, or that's comfortable for you. A friend is someone with whom you don't have secrets. A friend is someone you understand and accept as they are."

"Roger, I'm a little confused right now. What is your point?"

"My point is that if we're really going to be friends, there can't be a part of my life, a huge part of my life, that I can't talk about with you because it bothers you, or makes you uncomfortable, or that you find threatening. It shouldn't be that way. You're straight. You're not going to become gay by listening to me talk about men, any more than I'm going to become straight listening to you talk about women. On the other hand, you might become a little less ignorant and a lot more tolerant."

I winced, because I knew Roger was right. I also winced because I feared I was about to hear Roger tell me how good it feels to have a cock rammed up his ass, or how much he loves the taste of semen and sperm.

"Roger, this is hard for me."

"I understand that, Dave. It's difficult for all straight men. That's part of the problem. You've been so conditioned into a gag reflex that you've forgotten the essential truth that gay men are just like straight men when it comes to sex. It's as normal for us to fuck men as it's normal for you to fuck women. It's as normal for us to want to be fucked by a man as it is for you to be fucked by a woman. We fantasize about sex the same way you do. And we both like getting blown. Frankly, men are better at giving head than women, because we know what we want. I bet it's the same for lesbians."

"I'll have to take your word on the blow jobs. I don't know though, I've had women that understand exactly what I want and have had at me like I was their next meal."

I hesitated before continuing, because I was about to say things I never thought I would say to a gay man.

Roger nodded and seemed to understand my caution. But he insisted, "Go on, Dave. Say it."

"It's fucking filthy, Roger. Taking it up the ass is fucking filthy. Do you suck a cock that's been in your ass? Does someone suck yours? Does it taste like shit? That just sounds awful to me. Do you at least wear a condom or two? Do men bleed from the ass while you're fucking them? Oh god man, have you ever sucked a cock that has shit and blood on it? Don't fucking answer that question. I don't want to know. You know, a lot of people, well, straight people, think this new disease that's going around is because gay, male sex is completely unhygienic."

I paused and looked at Roger before saying, "I'm so sorry. That was really ugly."

Roger was nodding his head. "David, I knew you needed to say those things. Now I actually feel like we can talk. It is possible, you know, for a straight man and a gay man to be friends. As for all your questions, I think you already know the answers."

I said, "I'm glad we didn't talk about this before dinner."

"That's why I told you to eat first and then we'd chat."

"So you're not offended by everything I just said?"

Roger assured me. "I don't feel any worse than you do for having said it. I was bothered that we'd avoided talking about it before. Don't you feel better getting that off your chest?"

"Is it okay if I say no?"

"Of course."

"I suppose I do," I added doubtfully. "Give me a little time. You've dumped a lot on me here. I'm still getting used to your real voice. I need my mommy."

"I'm your mother today, David."

"Thank you," I said, "but Roger, wouldn't you and Tim be happier to simply be yourselves all the time, without the affectations?"

"Probably," Roger admitted. "But the affectations can also be really fun. You've seen that. And . . . they're a magnet for all the young studs fresh into town, especially at the baths."

"So then, you and Tim aren't monogamous."

"No, not quite. Not yet, anyway. We've talked about it, though. I swear the problem is Hilary. He's such a slut and constantly introducing us to these horny guys."

"What about Terry? Aren't they still together?"

Roger looked at me seriously. He said, "David, Terry is sick and Hilary won't touch him anymore."

"Well that's rude," I said with irritation.

Roger sighed and said, "You're right, it is rude, and despicable, but he's also probably pretty smart. It looks like Terry has that new sickness."

I sincerely said, "I'm sorry."

There was a fairly long pause before Roger continued. "It's getting to be a scary time, David. More and more people are becoming sick and no one knows why. I think it's going to get a lot worse before it gets better."

"Great," I said. "That's all the world needs. Another reason to be antagonistic toward gay people. I'm really sorry about what I said earlier."

"I got news for you, sweetie," Roger advised. "I don't think gays are the only ones that are going to get sick. So are the straights."

"Really?" I shuddered at the thought.

Roger nodded.

"Straight sex? Not just anal sex?"

Roger said, "Any sex."

I whined, "Thank you for giving me the all time erection killer."

"You're welcome."

"You mean it's time for me to settle down?"

"Are you ready for that?"

I considered the question, and not for the first time.

Roger asked, "Cynthia's not the one?"

"No, I don't think so. Not as long as she's into that weird shit. It's a wall between us."

Roger advised, "You better let her go then, before you're in too deep and can't leave without a huge mess." Then he asked, "What about the dyke? What's her name?"

"Are you talking about Gwen?"

"Yeah, I've heard you talk about her with your roommate. Don't you two have some huge unrequited boner for each other?"

"Yeah, we do."

"Well?"

"Number one, even though she says she might be moving back, Gwen doesn't live here. Number two, she's bisexual, not just a dyke, you asshole, and she has a pretty low opinion of most men. Number three, the biggest issue between us is timing. Our timing is as bad as our phone sex is great. I'd love to work it out with Gwen. I think you would adore her. But on the other hand, and maybe I'm naïve here, working it out isn't what I'm looking for. That's true with Cynthia, too. I don't want to work it out. I want it to be right from the start. I want to meet someone, fall in love, and live happily ever after. I want that so much."

"You're ready for monogamy?"

"Yes. I've been monogamous with Cynthia."

"I guess that doesn't include the phone sex with Gwen."

I argued, "That's not the same, but I know what you mean. Yes, I am ready to settle down. I believe in love. My parents are in love. I was in love once, I think. I want to be in love again. I've been knocked off my feet a few times. Roger, there was this one woman at State, an actress named Annette. I swear my entire body became a hard-on when I looked at her."

"Ah yes, the innocence of true love. No doubt you would have swept her off her feet had she known the purity of your affection."

I challenged Roger. "Okay smart ass, shouldn't you and Tim try a little harder to be monogamous?"

"Yes."

"And?"

"We're working on it."

"You're supposed to be making me feel better, Roger. You're not supposed to be making me worry about you. I'm the one that's supposed to be getting mothered today."

"I am so sorry. What was I thinking?"

"You were thinking about why you have to talk like a fag and how you prefer talking like a man. Then you decided to give me a crash course in gay awareness and friendship, while allowing me the cathartic opportunity to clearly and succinctly express a short list of homophobic revulsions."

Roger nodded and smiled. "The thing is, Dave, most gay people are just like anyone and that's the way it should be. I guarantee you there are people you know right now that are gay and they act totally straight. Some of them haven't come out yet, but some of them have and you simply can't tell, because they don't act a certain way. You'd be surprised, Dave. We're not all swishy. You're just used to the Castro boys, and let's face it, for straights, the stereotype is easier to digest."

I asked, "How do you know that about other gay people?"

"Because I've been gay my entire life and I know gay people everywhere. By the way, I see straight people that act gayer than anyone in the Castro and vice versa. We're all just people, despite the stereotypes. In fact, I think the sooner we can get away from the stereotypes, the better it will be for everyone."

"Thanks for coming over today, Roger."

"You don't want me to leave yet, do you?"

"No, I just wanted to thank you."

"You're welcome, David."

"What do you want to do now?"

"I brought over a movie."

"What did you bring?"

"The Way We Were."

"I don't care much for her, but I adore him."

"I knew it. Me too. See David," he lisped, "just a chromosome or two . . ."

"Stop it. Make some more tea. I'm going to call my mother."

"Tell her I said hello."

Final Project for Speech 551

Carl: Good afternoon, ladies and gentlemen, welcome to the Wide, Wild World of Sports. I'm Carl Badwig and we're on the campus of San Francisco State University, specifically in one of the classrooms in the department of Speech and Communication. This is an institution that is no stranger to controversy, and, as such, is a fitting venue for this program. We are here today to discuss and debate the various issues surrounding the so-called 1st Gay Games, or as they were originally called, the 1st Gay Olympic Games, scheduled to be held in late August here in the beautiful city of San Francisco. We have several distinguished guests on the dais prepared to present and examine their points of view in what has increasingly become a contentious topic.

From my left to right, we have Dr. Cynthia Appease, the first openly lesbian tenured professor in the United States here at San Francisco State. She is also a teacher of sexual roles and behavior in contemporary society.

Next, we have Tim Yu Hoo, an openly gay man and one of the nearly fifteen hundred athletes slated to participate in the Games.

Next is Jessica Pettit, one of the many volunteers from San Francisco Arts and Athletics who are putting this event together.

Then we have the Reverend David Straight, a Protestant minister in San Francisco and an outspoken critic of both these Games and of homosexuality as a lifestyle.

Next to the Reverend, we have Connie Noble, representing the point of view of the United States Olympic Committee.

And, finally, one of the great entertainers of our time, and I'm proud to add, an old friend of mine, Sherrice Burner, who has agreed to perform at the opening ceremonies.

I, of course, am here to moderate this event, but through the course of research and investigation, I have formed my own opinions and will, from time to time, insert them into this dialogue. I realize this makes me something other than an unbiased journalist, but some issues call for non-partisan facilitation and others call for a person to take a stand. In my opinion, this is an issue that demands a stance. I promise, however, to be as professional as possible.

Before we open this issue to discussion from our guests, it would be helpful to give some background information to our audience members who are hearing about this for the first time. Dr. Tom Waddell, a man who is intimately familiar with both the Olympic Games and controversy, originally conceived the Gay Games. In 1968, he was a member of the United States team that competed in the 19th Summer Games, held in Mexico City. He finished in 6th place in the decathlon, an outstanding achievement in and of itself. Further, he posted a score of 7,719 points, which was a personal best. He also was a strong vocal supporter of the black athletes who almost boycotted those games. The possible consequences of that support are one of the issues we will be discussing today.

In 1980, Dr. Waddell came up with the idea of the Gay Olympic Games and then formed San Francisco Arts and Athletics, a nonprofit organization. Along with Dr. Waddell, a committee of homosexual men and women have worked tirelessly for two years on a shoestring budget with a staff of volunteers to bring his vision to fruition. Everything seemed to be moving into place for the event until January of this year, when the United States Olympic Committee threatened legal action against San Francisco Arts and Athletics and Dr. Waddell personally, unless they drop the word Olympic from the event.

Due to a conflict in schedule, Dr. Waddell could not join us today, but we are delighted to have Ms. Jessica Pettit, one of the volunteers from San Francisco Arts and Athletics. Ms. Pettit, can you give us additional information regarding your organization and an update on the status of the event?

Jessica: Thank you; I'd love to, Mr. Badwig.

Carl: Just Carl, please. That goes for everyone.

Jessica: Well, Carl, it is my distinct pleasure to tell you the 1st Gay Olympic Games, and Gay Cultural Week, will begin on August 28 of this year and run until September 5.

Connie: Pardon me for interrupting, but please don't call it Olympic.

Carl: Pardon me, Ms. Noble. You will be afforded your full complement of time when it is your turn. Until such time, I ask you to refrain from interrupting whomever is speaking and whatever their particular point of view. Please continue, Ms. Pettit.

Jessica: Thank you. As I was saying, everything is on schedule and will take place exactly as envisioned. Despite the efforts of the USOC to undermine us, athletes and artists from around the world are coming to San Francisco to participate in both aspects of this celebration.

Carl: While I understand Gay Cultural Week is to be a vital part of the event, I would ask you to keep your remarks focused on the athletic competition, since that is the source of the controversy, and this, of course, is a sports program.

Jessica: I understand, Carl. It's interesting that you call it an athletic competition. I suppose, in the narrowest terms it is that. But Dr. Tom Waddell's vision for this is less about competition and more about doing your personal best, whether you win or lose. Everyone who competes is a winner.

Carl: That's quite admirable. What events constitute these games?

Jessica: There are seventeen total sports. They are Basketball, Billiards, Bowling, Boxing, Cycling, Golf, Marathon, Physique or Body Building, Powerlifting, Rugby, Soccer, Softball, Swimming and Diving, Tennis, Track and Field, Volleyball, and Wrestling.

Carl: Are all these sports open to both men and women?

Jessica: I'm glad you asked that, because we feel that's one of the more unique elements to these games. All sports are for both sexes, except Rugby, which is for women only, and Wrestling, which is for men only. However, five of the sports are for men, women, and coed teams. Those are Billiards, Golf, Swimming and Diving, Tennis, and Track and Field. We're extremely excited about the coed sports and we're hoping to expand those for the 2nd Gay Olympic Games.

Carl: And where will these events take place?

Jessica: In venues all over the city and Bay area, but the opening and closing ceremonies, along with Track and Field, will be at Kezar Stadium.

Carl: How many athletes are you anticipating?

Jessica: We will have somewhere in the neighborhood of 1500 athletes, from 12 countries and counting, and close to 180 cities will be represented from around the world.

Carl: How were these athletes selected?

Jessica: They weren't selected. They volunteered. All ages, races, and abilities are welcome.

Carl: No requirements at all?

Jessica: None whatsoever, Carl.

Carl: How large is the pool of volunteers working for San Francisco Arts and Athletics?

Jessica: I don't have the exact figure on that, but I think it's around 600 people. Though in truth, the number of volunteers who consistently take part is much smaller.

Carl: What is your budget for the event?

Jessica: Again, I don't have the exact total, but my understanding is a little over $100, 000.

Carl: That seems like a preposterously small amount of money for what you are attempting to accomplish. How much is your organization prepared to lose, financially speaking, on this venture?

Jessica: It's true that our budget is low, but I don't think we're prepared to lose anything. We're determined, at the very worst, to break even.

Carl: Jessica, how can this be possible?

Jessica: San Francisco is an amazing place. People have been contributing in all sorts of ways, not just financial. In fact, most contributions have not been monetary. Office equipment has been donated. People have brought tables and chairs. We've been given copy and fax machines, staplers, phones, you name it.

Carl: What kind of fundraising has been done? It sounds like there hasn't been much with a budget that small.

Jessica: Well, I think we got a late start on that, and I know that in the future we will be much more proactive. Remember, we've only had two years to put this all together, from idea to reality. We'll have four years next time, along with all the experience we've gained. But again, people in this city have been fantastic. On the most basic, grassroots level, people have found ways to raise the money we've needed. From bake sales, spaghetti feeds, T-shirt sales, raffles, all sorts of things. And we have had contributions, from the Club Baths of San Francisco and a sizeable donation from the Club Bath Chain of Miami. There's still time for others to contribute. The word is getting out. Finally, as many of you know, next week, on Saturday, May 22, there will begin the coast-to-coast National Torch Run. It will start in New York, from the Stonewall area of Greenwich Village, and proceed along a northerly route and include Chicago, Minneapolis, Des Moines, and Denver, to name just a few. Joggers and cyclists will carry the torch and there will be many fundraising events along the way. It will culminate with the lighting of the Olympic flame at the opening ceremonies.

Carl: Most impressive Ms. Pettit. I'll be back with you in a few minutes, but right now I'd like to turn our attention to others on the panel, starting with you, Ms. Connie Noble. Ms. Noble, why is the United States Olympic Committee determined to disallow use of the word Olympic for these Gay Games?

Connie: Quite simply, Carl, we're upholding the law. It is illegal for San Francisco Arts and Athletics to use the word Olympic for any event they choose to hold.

Carl: And to what law are you referring?

Connie: I am referring to the Amateur Sports Act, Federal Law 95606, passed by Congress in 1978. This law designates the United States Olympic Committee as the coordinating body for all Olympic related athletic activity in the United States.

Carl: So then, it is the position of the USOC that by using the word Olympic, San Francisco Arts and Athletics is in violation of that law.

Connie: Clearly.

Carl: And you are prepared to pursue this matter to the fullest extent of the law?

Connie: Without question.

Carl: To the best of your knowledge, Ms. Noble, are there any other mitigating factors influencing the USOC pursuant to this matter?

Connie: None that I'm aware.

Carl: That being your position, Ms. Noble, what say you to the rather highly contentious relationship between the USOC's executive director, Colonel F. Don Miller, and Dr. Tom Waddell, the chairman of San Francisco Arts and Athletics?

Connie: I'm sorry, but I'm not privy to the dynamics of their relationship, contentious or otherwise.

Carl: Have you seen the correspondence between the two?

Connie: I have not, though their correspondence has been summarized for me and my understanding is that those letters are at least part of the basis for potential litigation. It is the position of the USOC that within that documentation, an agreement was reached to drop the word Olympic from association with this event.

Carl: We'll leave that to the courts, Ms. Noble. But I just want to be clear here on something. Are you unaware of the personal conflict between Colonel Miller and Dr. Waddell that began during the Games of the 19th Olympiad in Mexico City?

Connie: I have never discussed or overheard discussion regarding any personal conflict between Colonel Miller, or any other member of the USOC, and Dr. Waddell.

Carl: Then allow me to inform you and our audience that the rift between Colonel Miller and Dr. Waddell has very deep roots. During the Games of Mexico City, following the civil rights protest of African-American athletes Tommie Smith and John Carlos on the medal stand after the 200-meter dash, Tom Waddell came out in strong vocal support for his teammates and the treatment of all the African-American athletes. Dr. Waddell said, and I quote, "I was pleased by their protest. I was afraid they weren't going to do it. I was disappointed more Negro athletes backed down." Then when Dr. Waddell was asked if the athletes' actions had discredited the American flag, he said, "I think they have been discredited by the flag more often than they have discredited it." And finally, when he was asked if the US image had been tarnished, Dr. Waddell replied, "Our image is so bad it can't get any worse. Maybe this will help." Then, during the middle of the decathlon competition, a representative of Colonel Miller approached Dr. Waddell, who was in the Army at the time, and threatened him with a court-martial. Given the weight of that threat, which proved to be nothing more than the empty threats of a common bully, it is all the more remarkable that Dr. Waddell achieved his own personal best score in the decathlon. Ms. Noble, you're telling me you've never heard about any of this?

Connie: Okay, I have heard a little about this, but this has nothing to do with the issues regarding the Gay Games.

Carl: Is that a fact?

Connie: To the best of my knowledge, yes.

Carl: We may come back to this issue, because I feel it bears scrutiny in this matter. But there is another facet that deserves to be explored here and for which the USOC should be called to question, and that is the issue of discrimination. Ms. Noble, besides any personal vendetta between Colonel Miller and Dr. Waddell, isn't the real issue here the fact that the word Olympic is being used in conjunction with an event that celebrates the entire worldwide homosexual community?

Connie: That is completely false, Carl. That is an outrageous allegation and serves only to cloud the facts in this situation. The use of the word Olympic for this event is a clear violation of the law. That is our only complaint.

Carl: Is that a fact, Ms. Noble?

Connie: Yes.

Carl: And yet, Ms. Noble, while the USOC pursues this matter with what you consider righteous vigor, isn't it also true the USOC has turned a blind eye again and again to other organizations that hold events similar to these, using the allegedly protected word of Olympic as part of their title?

Connie: I am aware there have been some exceptions.

Carl: Some?

Connie: A few.

Carl: Only a few?

Connie: I'm sorry, I don't have an exact list in front of me right now.

Carl: Well then, allow me to enlighten and inform you and our audience to at least a partial list of organizations that have been granted the freedom, or in many cases, simply have been ignored, while they not only use the name Olympic, but also do so without any permission from the USOC. The list reads: Junior Olympics, Special Olympics, Wheelchair Olympics, Police Olympics, Fireman Olympics, K-9 Olympics, Armenian Olympics, Xerox Olympics, Crab Cooking Olympics, Diaper Olympics, Rat Olympics, Nude Olympics, Kidney Transplant Olympics, and then my two favorites, Alcoholic Olympics and Recovered Alcoholic Olympics. Ms. Noble, are you aware of all these events prominently and freely using the word Olympic?

Connie: I am aware of a few of them, but not all that you just listed.

Carl: Indeed, Ms. Noble. And what say the USOC that they should allow all these events and yet not find them in violation of the seemingly sacred Amateur Sports Act, passed by Congress in 1978?

Connie: I can't speak to each of these events, but I believe the general consensus is that these events could never be confused with the actual Olympic Games, whereas an event called the Gay Olympic Games might confuse the public.

Carl: Are you serious? Is that really the position of the USOC?

Connie: I think I'm speaking a little out of turn here. I'd rather just leave it that in the view of the USOC, the use of the word Olympic in the case of San Francisco Arts and Athletics is illegal.

Carl: Very well, Ms. Noble, we'll be back to you in a few minutes. I'd like to turn our attention now to one of the athletes participating in these Games. Mr. Tim Yu Hoo, how do you do?

Tim: Very well, Carl; it's an honor to meet you.

Carl: You are most kind. What is your event in these games?

Tim: Track and Field. Specifically, I will run the hurdles.

Carl: Have you ever run competitively before?

Tim: Yes, in high school.

Carl: What made you decide to compete again?

Tim: Because I love the idea of these games. That winning and losing are not the reasons to participate. That doing your best is the ultimate victory. But that's not all.

Carl: Go on.

Tim: Thank you. Aside from that ideal, what appeals to me most about these games is that they bring the entire gay community together and they serve to puncture the popular mythology of stereotypes that are both demeaning and limiting.

Carl: Please elaborate.

Tim: I hope I am allowed to say this, but one of the most frustrating aspects of being a gay man is that we are all perceived as being, please excuse my language, limp-wristed faggots. We are not all this way. In fact, very few are actually this most popular and annoying stereotype. Most homosexuals I know, both male and female, are no different in appearance and behavior from any heterosexual.

Carl: That is a fascinating and enlightening point of view. I can tell that you are excited about participating in these games.

Tim: These games have changed my life. Before I heard about them, I had not openly admitted to anyone that I am homosexual. I held this inside me since I was a boy, because I did not see where I fit in. I am not flamboyant. I am shy. But I love sports, all sports. I love baseball and football, but always, always I have loved track and field the most.

Carl: Why?

Tim: I am a fast runner, but more than that, there is a component to track and field that is different from team sports. In track and field, you first compete against yourself and then your opponent. Also, unlike team sports, my coaches never taught me to hate my opponent. I only had to run faster or not. And unlike team sports, I often found my opponent did not hate me. We were always happy for one another when we found we had done our personal best. I have missed that in my life. Now, I can have that again and be openly gay, and be surrounded by gay people from all over the world who feel as I do. You have no idea what this means to me. I feel I am a man, a human being, with a place in this world where I belong. I believe the opening ceremonies will be the greatest moment so far, in my entire life.

Carl: As you can see, ladies and gentlemen, several on this dais are moved, myself included. Dr. Cynthia Appease, as an openly homosexual person and professor of sexual roles and behavior in our society, what is your take on these issues?

Cynthia: Thank you, Carl. I am deeply moved and inspired by what Mr. Yu Hoo just said. I am so inspired, in fact, I think I'd like to take this opportunity right now and announce that I am going to compete in these games as well.

Carl: What will be your event?

Cynthia: I was on the diving team in high school and I think it's time for me to dive again. Thank you, Tim. You have inspired me.

Tim: You are most welcome.

Carl: Just a wonderful moment. Dr. Appease, what are your other impressions so far?

Cynthia: I'm thrilled by the concept of the Gay Olympic Games. I'd like to expand on something Tim touched on, and that is how these games are bringing the entire gay community together. This is not a casual issue. The gay community, for far too long, has been splintered, perhaps even fractured, along sexual lines. There has been a huge division between women and men. Many gay women I know have a deep-seated distrust of men in general, and that includes gay men. Just as society works best when we are all working together, so too does the gay community and, in fact, this event could be a turning point, both real and symbolic, in the struggle for equality between the sexes.

And the timing could not be better. The gay community of San Francisco has been on the rise for the past several years. In fact, our political clout is being viewed as a model for cities around the world. That's why it makes so much sense for the 1st Gay Olympic Games to be held in San Francisco. On top of all that, there is the single fact that this event, be it called Olympic or not, will be the largest gathering ever, to date, of homosexual people in a single place. The symbolic magnitude of that and the very real credibility, sociologically speaking, cannot be overstated. On the other hand, I am appalled, and yet not at all surprised, by the position of the USOC regarding the Gay Olympic Games. Their denial of homosexuality as an issue in this matter is weak and transparent. But it's not a shock. This is the world we live in. Homophobia permeates every element of our society, even as the gay community systematically breaks down barrier after barrier. As each barrier is crossed, the homophobe clings ever tighter and more desperately to the last vestiges of what they hold to be true. Homophobia also offers further proof of how evolution is a slow, painful process.

Carl: Please elaborate on that.

Cynthia: Homosexuality is nothing new. This is not simply a San Francisco or 20th century phenomenon. It is ironic that such a fuss is being made about the Olympics. The Olympics were founded in Greece, in the year 776 BC, at a time when homosexuality was both commonplace and accepted. The only event that year was a sprint around 200 yards, I believe, and all the participants were nude. Can you imagine the scandal if an event took place in the nude today?

Carl: Except, apparently, for the Nude Olympics.

Cynthia: You're right. Also, since those first Olympics were dedicated to Zeus, women were not allowed to compete. So in certain ways, the modern Olympics have both progressed and regressed. But the Gay Olympics are clearly an attempt to evolve into a higher model.

Carl: What do you mean by that?

Cynthia: Both within society in general and within the gay community, there are stereotypes that need to be addressed. Tim made that point very well.

Carl: So then, Dr. Appease, if homosexuality was at one time a more accepted lifestyle behavior, what happened that it should be deemed verboten by the majority of society?

Cynthia: Well, like any minority point of view, homosexuality has always had its detractors. But if you're looking for one event that caused public sentiment to swing wildly in a homophobic direction, it was the publishing of the Bible, both the Old and then New Testaments.

Carl: I caution you, Dr. Appease, you are traveling on a slippery slope right now. As a Jew, I am entirely familiar with what is called the Old Testament. But as I am not familiar with the New Testament, this is an opportune time to bring in another of our panel to join this discussion, the Reverend David Straight.

David: Hello Carl, thank you for allowing me to be a part of this discussion.

Carl: Are you in agreement with Dr. Appease that the Bible fanned the flames of homophobia?

David: No, I don't think the Bible fanned any flames. Actually, the Bible cleared the air, and made quite plain the view of God regarding homosexuality. It is against God's law. That includes the Old and New Testaments.

Carl: I see. And what is your view on the matter of the Gay Olympic Games?

David: Well, of course I am not equipped to discuss the legal dispute between the conflicting organizations. I am only able to speak with authority regarding the morality, or lack thereof, of any such assembly celebrating an abomination of God's law.

Carl: Ladies and gentlemen, I ask you to please refrain from any outbursts. The Reverend has volunteered his time today and I give him high marks for walking into the belly of the beast, as it were, to openly present his point of view. He has waited patiently and should be afforded his full say. I apologize to you, Reverend Straight. Please continue.

David: Thank you, Carl, and God bless all of you here today. I am prepared to agree with Dr. Appease, when she stated that homosexuality has been part of our world far longer than the existence of the Bible, or even any recognition of the one, true God. The same can be said for all sin, since the Garden of Eden. But the Bible, being the word of God, is the one inerrant truth in these matters and there is no debate regarding the Bible's stance on homosexuality.

Carl: Is that so? To which passage or passages in the Bible do you refer, or find the most persuasive for your position?

David: Of course, there are several, but clearly the lessons of Sodom and Gomorrah are absolute in their condemnation of this abomination. It is, of course, where the word sodomite is derived and consequently reviled.

Carl: I've heard this argument from Christian theologians before, but I want to be sure we're clear here. . . . You're saying the sin of Sodom that brought the destruction of God's wrath on that city was homosexuality?

David: Yes, that is correct.

Carl: This has always been interesting to me, because as a Jew I remember vividly a discussion in temple regarding Genesis chapter 19 when I was a boy. My teacher, a great man, Rabbi Mordecai Shpladt, had a different interpretation of these events that included homosexuality, but not as the exclusive source of

God's wrath and absolutely not as a definitive statement against homosexuality.

David: Well, I'm sorry, but . . .

Carl: As well you should be sir, for interrupting me. Now, as I was saying, my Rabbi viewed God's wrath regarding Sodom and Gomorrah as due to many factors, including rape, as well as a lack of charity toward strangers and the poor. The behavior of those people was not exclusively directed at the house of Lot and the angels he welcomed as guests within. It was a pervasive pattern throughout the region and that is why God smote all the people: men, women, and children. And while it is possible to infer that God had no great love for homosexual behavior, it is also possible that this feeling was directed exclusively toward those who rape or prostitute themselves, be they homo or heterosexual. Furthermore, if the events in Genesis are taken literally, God's wrath was caused by the threat of rape toward two of his angels that were visiting the house of Lot, and as such do not even qualify as homosexual rape, but bestial rape, as angels are not human. Clearly, this would qualify as abomination. On this, there is no dispute in the Bible.

David: While I may not entirely agree with your interpretation, or rather, your Rabbi's interpretation, it is clear you know your Old Testament.

Carl: To a Jew sir, what you call the Old Testament is the Bible. Perhaps your point of view would be better served by sticking with the New Testament, of which I know very little.

David: I understand. However, I consider myself a scholar of both Testaments. So I would love to hear your or your rabbi's interpretation of the clearest and simplest reference in the Bible to the condemnation of homosexuality, Leviticus 18:22, *"Thou shalt not lie with mankind, as with womankind: it is abomination."*

Carl: As you wish, Reverend. My first observation is that you are using the most popular modern translation, from the King James Bible, and not the literal translation, as it was first written in

Hebrew which says, *"And with a male you shall not lay lyings of a woman."* I'm sure you will agree those are two entirely different statements and open to interpretations that vary in no small matter. While the conservative Christian interpretation of your translation seems entirely clear, the original text—especially within the context of Leviticus, which deals mostly with sins of man against woman, idolatry, and to a lesser degree bestiality—may offer entirely different interpretations. For example, in its original form that verse may be saying that a man may not lie with another man in a woman's bed, for that bed is sacred to woman. It might also refer to ritual sex between two men in a Pagan temple, something not uncommon to the time that was also forbidden. As for Rabbi Shpladt, he said the problem with that particular verse is that it's unclear exactly what it means. He could not, nor could anyone else, decipher the exact meaning of the phrase, *"lay lyings."* In the King James translation you quote, along with every other modern translation I've read, the original text is changed to suit your own slant and has no place being called the true word of the Bible as it was originally written. I want to add one more comment on the Bible and homosexuality as it pertained to my beloved Rabbi. He once said that while the Bible seems to frown upon acts of sex between man and man, nowhere in the Bible does it condemn a loving, nurturing sexual relationship between consenting adults. Nowhere.

Cynthia: Carl, may I interject something here, please?

Carl: As long as it's brief, because I have not given the Reverend a chance to respond or have his complete say.

Cynthia: Thank you. I just want to add one more thought regarding homosexuality and the Bible. There is not a single reference to women having sex with women in the original text. Some of the newer translations that you referred to, and are commonly quoted by Christian theologians, liberally use the word homosexuality and they say that includes women. But the word homosexual was first used in the late 19th century. It never appears in the original Bible, Old or New Testaments.

Carl: You're right, you're right. You're absolutely correct.

Jessica: Excuse me, but exactly what does any of this have to do with the 1st Gay Olympic Games?

Connie: Please don't use the word Olympic.

Jessica: Up yours.

Carl: Ladies, please. There is no cause for that language or for rancor to ensue. The purpose, Ms. Pettit, of this aspect to our discussion, is to understand the reaction of a vast majority of the populous to the entire gay community and, by extension, the prospect of a so-called Gay Olympic Games.

Jessica: I apologize for the language, but not for questioning why we seem to have veered so far off course here. I thought you said this is a sports program. We need to get back to the real issues. With all due respect to the Bible, the Reverend, Rabbi Shpladt, and either ancient or contemporary translations, we don't live in the Biblical world, we live in the real world. In the real world, there always have been and always will be homosexuals. We are as much a part of the fabric of this planet, and have as much birthright to do as we please, as any other minority point of view and any people that live and breathe.

Sherrice: Here, here.

David: If I could be allowed to continue.

Carl: She's right. Ms. Pettit is right. I'm sorry, Reverend, but we have veered too far from the topic at hand. And, I must add, your point of view, however valid it is to you and your constituents, seems ill informed as it relates to the Old Testament. As such, your opinions regarding the New Testament are similarly suspect from the outset and, as Ms. Pettit so adroitly put it, have nothing to do with the 1st Gay Games. So turning our attention back to task, it is my pleasure to bring in an old friend who will very much be part of these games. Sherrice Burner, it's wonderful to see you again.

    Sherrice: It's always nice to see you, Carl.

    Carl: So you are to perform at the opening ceremonies. What compelled you to do this, when several other famous performing artists, and open homosexuals, turned down the invitation?

    Sherrice: First, Carl, there's no controversy about other artists. There were scheduling conflicts, plain and simple. I've talked to several of them and they all wanted to be here, but they simply can't. Not this time, anyway. But for me, it was easy. I don't have anything else scheduled and it's really a no-brainer. I mean, are you kidding me? There's going to be a stadium full of people in San Francisco. I can't wait to perform. I'm gonna be hot, baby. I've got a Bob Mackie dress that's about the size of a postage stamp. I'm gonna stretch that thing on and shake it.

    Carl: As only you can, Sherrice. And what are your impressions about the issues we've been discussing today?

    Sherrice: Well, as some of you may know, I am a Buddhist, but I was raised on the teachings of the Christian God. I think you touched on this, but the way the Bible is taught has changed over the years, in order to support a view against same-sex relationships. But in the teachings of Buddha, no such conflict exists.

    Carl: Are you saying that Buddhism supports a homosexual lifestyle?

    Sherrice: No, that's not what I said. There are five precepts to Buddhism and the third precept is to abstain from sexual misconduct. In all the Buddha's teachings, there is nothing to justify or condemn homosexuality. There is no sexual misconduct as long as there is mutual consent, no intentional harm is being done, no commitment to another person is being broken, and where the sole intention is to express affection with respect, and to give pleasure to each other. The key is being in a loving, nurturing, and committed relationship, not merely the hedonistic pursuit of any pleasure, be it sexual or not.

Carl: Do all Buddhists feel as you do?

Sherrice: Unfortunately, no. There are some, especially in countries where homosexuality is still deemed a crime, where the dominant culture has influenced Buddhist thought. But there is nothing in the teachings of Buddha that condemns any loving relationship.

Carl: What are you going to perform at the opening ceremony?

Sherrice: I'd rather not say. Let it be a surprise. Frankly, though I'm delighted and honored to be here, I'd like to hear more from the participants and the organizers. They're the real heroes.

Carl: Thank you, Sherrice. You are correct. The focus here needs to be on the Games and with that in mind, I would like to ask Jessica Pettit a couple of questions. Ms. Pettit, why is using the word Olympic so important to your organization? Wouldn't it be simpler if San Francisco Arts and Athletics dropped that word and let these games stand as their own separate entity?

Jessica: Perhaps it would be simpler, but the word Olympic is a significant symbol in contemporary culture. It represents an ideal of global inclusiveness. In every possible way, the 1st Gay Olympic Games stands for the same thing. In fact, we wish to expand the luster of that ideal by eliminating objective athletic standards for participation. We do not want age, race, creed, handicap, or lifestyle to dictate who can participate. There are people taking part in events they've never even tried before. They will receive training from those who are skilled in their events. They will compete with those of similar skill levels. There will be the traditional medals of gold, silver, and bronze, but the real winners merely have to take part and try their best. To take part is the Olympic ideal, not to win a medal. It is only our society that has placed such an emphasis on winning and losing. That's one of the reasons we do not agree with the USOC regarding their contention that our games may cause confusion with the "real" Olympics. I mean, get serious. We have athletic events that are different. We have criteria for involvement that's different. I don't recall seeing the Olympic Games with participants taking part in their events for the first time competitively. How can this possibly confuse the public? Lastly, regarding the word Olympic, there is the issue of free speech as protected by the constitution. San Francisco Arts and Athletics is a nonprofit organization. We are not looking to financially capitalize on the word Olympic. If all these other organizations you mentioned, and we support every one of them, can use the word Olympic, why can't we?

Carl: It's a fair question, and I'd like Ms. Connie Noble to address it. If there can be an Alcoholic Olympics or a Rat Olympics or, indeed, a Special Olympics, why can't there be a Gay Olympics?

Connie: It's against the law.

Carl: And the others mentioned are not against the law?

Connie: I'm not prepared to discuss other situations or events. I have not been briefed as to the relative facts of those cases.

Carl: And that's as far as you are prepared to go on these issues today?

Connie: I believe these issues will be best served and fully absorbed under the unbiased scrutiny of the judicial process. We'll let the courts decide.

Carl: Very well, Ms. Noble. That will conclude today's presentation, but before we take a few questions from members of the audience, I'd like to make a closing remark. While the courts may, indeed, decide the relative merits of these issues legally, I suggest they have no providence over the moral and ethical issues. Furthermore, it is my opinion that the USOC is shameful in their handling of this situation. I believe the executive director, Colonel F. Don Miller, has allowed his own personal beliefs, including his private vendetta with Dr. Tom Waddell, to cloud his judgment. I believe the actions of the USOC regarding this matter, to date, are discriminatory. They are the ignorant and hateful reflexes of an organization that does not wish to be associated with a lifestyle they find repugnant. In behaving this way, the USOC is ironically at odds with the following portion of the Olympic Creed, and I quote, "*The most important thing in the Olympics is not to win, but to take part, just as the most important thing in life is not the triumph, but the struggle. The essential thing is not to have conquered but to have fought well.*" In this matter, I say the USOC has failed to meet their own standard, but San Francisco Arts and Athletics has earned the gold medal.

That's all the time we have for our presentation, but with our remaining time we'd like to take a few questions from our audience, directed to any member of our distinguished dais.

(The following Q & A was recorded on cassette and then transcribed)

Dr. Randle: Thank you so much. That was wonderful. Could you tell us a little bit about your process? Who came up with this idea?

Tim: It was my idea.

Dr. Randle: Are you actually running in the Games?

Tim: Yes.

Dr. Randle: How did all of you come up with the characters you portrayed?

Cynthia: That took awhile, because some of us wanted to be a character other than the one we played.

Dr. Randle: How did you resolve those conflicts?

Dave: Mud wrestling.

(Loud laughter)

Dr. Randle: I see. So did each of you write your own parts?

Jessica: Each of us researched our own parts, but Dave wrote the script.

Dr. Randle: Dave, you wrote all that?

Dave: Well, yes, but I couldn't have written a word without the incredible bounty of information everyone in the group gave me. Everyone was responsible for his or her own character, but they also pitched in with research on other parts. There was more information, but there was no way to cram it all into an hour. I also have to say, until I heard Carl do his Cosell voice, I didn't know how to write it.

Dr. Randle: Yes, Carl, that was wonderful. When did you realize you could imitate Howard Cosell?

Carl: (with his natural lisp, and then morphing into the Cosell voice) The first time I heard him speak was when I was a boy. Actually, I owe Howard Cosell my life. Boys in my neighborhood used to beat me up, until they heard me do that voice. After that, not only would they not beat me up, they would beat up anyone else that tried.

Dr. Randle: How fortunate for you, and where did you get that wig?

Carl: From one of Dave's friends.

Dr. Randle: Well the whole thing was just great. Anyone else have questions?

Vince (class member): Yeah, I got a couple of questions. First, since this is for gay people only, how do you know they're gay? Do you have some homo test? You know, cock sucking for men and bush munching for women? I mean, how do you know?

(Some laughter is heard from a few class members)

Jessica: You asshole.

Connie: I swear to god, I know where you park your fucking bike.

Vince: Oh that's nice. A threat. Everyone heard that. Butchie just threatened my motorcycle.

Carl: What an asshole.

Dave: To answer your question, there is no test. And no one said it was only for gay people. Anyone who enters an event is allowed the privilege and is treated with the same respect as everyone else. You could even enter an event, Vince. Who knows? You might make a few new friends.

Vince: No thanks. I'll be doing my nails during the Gay Olympics.

Connie: Don't use the word Olympic.

(Many people laugh)

Brian (class member): No disrespect intended, but since this is an athletic event, I'm trying to understand the lure of watching nonathletes compete in sports they may or may not have ever tried before. I mean, I'm a huge sports fan. I'll watch just about anything, but this sort of sounds like it might get embarrassing, at times at least, to watch. Again, I mean no disrespect.

Tim: It's a valid point and one that will have to be judged at the time. There's no way to know the caliber of athletes until the event is happening. However, my sense is that there are better athletes in the gay community than you are assuming.

Dave: Maybe another way of looking at it is how you feel when you're walking by a playground and there's a really competitive game of basketball or any sport that catches your eye. Do you stop and watch?

Brian: Sometimes, yeah. But I don't have to pay to watch guys in the neighborhood.

Dave: How about this? Have you ever watched an event and thought, I could do better than that?

Brian: Sure.

Dave: Well, the people in these games are going to have the courage to actually try to do better than that. And I agree with Tim that the caliber and quality might be much higher than anyone anticipates. Dr. Tom Waddell is not the only former Olympian that's going to compete in these games and I'm certain there are athletes out there who will welcome the chance to test their mettle against a former Olympian.

Brian: Okay, we'll see.

Vince: You couldn't fucking pay me to watch.

Several People: Shut up!

Gretchen (class member): I have a question. Is everything you presented true?

Several Group Members: Yes.

Gretchen: How come I don't read about this event or hear about it on the news?

Sherrice: That's a question we've been asking a lot as well.

Jessica: Yeah, other than the gay publications, there hasn't been much press.

Connie: The truth is the threat of a lawsuit from the USOC has brought more attention to the event than anything else.

Gretchen: How can that be? This is important.

Vince: Yeah, I'm shocked.

Dave: There's your answer. There are still a lot of scared, ignorant, narrow-minded, cement-headed cretins in the world.

Cynthia: You have to remember that San Francisco is not like most places. There's a history of tolerance here.

Tim: No. It's more than that. To say that gay people are tolerated is to imply there is a reason for tolerance. We are not tolerated by straights any more than we tolerate straights. We simply are. But it's also more than that. We're running things. Look at the elections. If a candidate gets our support, they get elected. If a measure or proposition gets our support, it gets passed and put into law. It's true that in many other places, we don't have such influence. But the world is changing and when the history books are written 100 years from now, 1,000 years from now, from this point forward, they will say the change took root in San Francisco. For the rest of our lives, we can say we were here when it happened. There's nothing anyone can do, especially the cretins of the world. They will either grow and evolve like the rest of us, or they will remain left behind in a puddle of bitterness. They will become more and more alone, hunting and clinging to nostalgic scraps of what went wrong that line their cupboards like roaches.

(Huge applause from audience. Vince gets up, flips off the class, and leaves. More huge applause.)

Connie: Damn, Tim. That was fucking great.

Tim: I feel so happy.

Dr. Randle: On that note, there's only one more thing I'd like to add to this excellent presentation and then class is dismissed. About fifteen minutes before the start of class, I received a phone call from a man named Roger, who is a friend of yours, Dave. He told me that he spoke with your mother and she told him to tell you the test results are negative. The tumor is benign. It was cat scratch fever.

(Very loud applause, laughter, and cheering ensue, though above the din, Jessica's voice could clearly be heard saying, "Cat scratch fever? Oh man, that song sucks.")

Two Cents' Worth

I was wet, cold, tired, and hungry. The long walk had not relieved my frustration. In fact, fatigue was compounding my reasons for taking the walk in the first place. I had left the apartment in haste and anger. I forgot to bring my wallet or apartment key. Luckily, I left the door unlocked. All I had were two pennies in my pocket. I don't know how long they'd been there, but it was at least since before the last time I did laundry.

I fingered them as I walked, occasionally noticing the copper scent when I used my right hand to wipe water from my face. The rain started while I sat at the western edge of Crissy Field, staring at the Golden Gate Bridge being enveloped by the darkening of misty twilight. The mist gave way to fat drops and I began walking home. That's when I discovered I hadn't brought my wallet. I wanted to stop at that little Italian restaurant at Fillmore and Chestnut, and hopefully wait out the storm. At least I could dry off a little. I was also craving a garlic, fresh clam, and parmesan pizza.

Despite spending at least an hour staring at the bridge, a sight that almost always made me feel better, I could not shake my mood. Earlier today, Cynthia came over and laid it out for me. She is leaving San Francisco soon after the first of the year, 1983, for El Cajon, a little town east of San Diego and barely north of the Mexican border. That's where the PRENARIUS Center is located. She will work after graduation, save her money, spend one more Christmas at home, and then be gone. She is going to forgo graduate school and continue her education there. She is being called to a higher source of learning. That's what she told me. I told her she needed a higher source of fiber and then maybe she could get all this bullshit out of her system.

I could no longer pretend to be supportive in our conversation, though her decision is not a surprise. She's been leaning that way since we met. We'd argued about it before, but it wasn't until today that I unleashed my full skepticism and ridicule. Even her own family, who'd gotten her into this cult, is calling it a crock. But that hasn't swayed Cynthia and I fear I'm going to lose her.

As I walked, I also had to consider if this is a bad thing. Do I even love her anymore? Given the difference between us, spiritually speaking, I don't know why she loves me. Maybe our relationship has run its course and this is the natural breaking point. It has certainly gone longer than any previous relationship I've had. And before Cynthia, any woman that expressed rigid belief in a spiritual dogma was my cue to exit. It didn't matter to me whether it was God, Werner Erhardt, L. Ron Hubbard, Buddha, Allah, the Swami Rugrash Rum Raisin, or those fucking Mormons that knock on my door. Come to think of it, though, the Latter Day Saints haven't been back since the time I saw them through the peephole, quickly stripped off everything but my socks, and opened the door. Using only my mind, I summoned the rise of my flagpole to a full, purple mountain majesty while extending my arms toward them saying, "Hello, I'd like to introduce **you** to the kingdom of God."

They stood frozen, and were at least momentarily incapable of responding. So I casually asked, "Seriously, how many wives do you think I could fetch with this?"

They scrambled down the stairs, almost climbing over one another, though one of the women looked back with something other than horror.

I guess, through all this time I've spent with Cynthia, I always considered PRENARIUS so weird and flaky that it wasn't a threat. Certainly, she never pressured me to believe as she believes. She completely understands my skepticism, because at one time she felt the same way. But a few months ago, when her parents told her they no longer believed, I could not understand why she held on. I still don't understand.

Today, she told me her decision and invited me to come with her. I can't tell if she wants to convert me, or have me save her. Frankly, I don't know if either one of those things is likely to happen. She said she loves me, and hopes I join her in El Cajon, but completely understands if I stay in San Francisco. The decision is entirely up to me.

I did not react well. It was probably the worst argument we've had. I don't want to write about the things we said. Our argument isn't the reason I'm writing now, either. Suffice to say we didn't break up, but we didn't make up. She left hurt, and soon after, I made my hasty departure.

So I was walking home hungry, wet, and tired. I was thinking about the day, the relationship, and the recent news from Gwen that she is saving her money for a return to the Bay Area sometime next year. Our phone conversations have become more frequent again, and our friendship has only grown stronger.

I made it all the way to Fort Mason and was taking a shortcut across the grass. Everything was soaked, including me, so there was no reason to stay on the pavement. Even though I was tired, most of the long walk was behind me. I felt a slight energy renewal and I think I was picking up the pace. I looked down at my feet and the noise my shoes were making through the long, wet grass.

I guess that's why I didn't hear anyone approach me, nor did I see what suddenly smashed me over the back of the head. I remember hitting the ground and then several rough hands turned me over and searched me. I could not focus enough to see how many there were, but I do remember a voice saying, "Two cents? That's all he's got?"

I think I laughed, or maybe I wanted to laugh and made some other sound. The one thing I know for sure is they started kicking me. I don't know how many times. At some point, I passed out. It was still raining when I came to. I tasted blood in my mouth. When I tried to move, I couldn't. I lay awhile longer and think I blacked out again. Finally, I tested my limbs and gradually realized I could probably get up. It was a slow process. It took me at least five minutes to get to one knee. My head and ribs were aching. I stood up. I was dizzy and almost fell. I don't know how long I stood and attempted to harness what remained of my senses and strength. Eventually, I took a step. I took another step. I swallowed a mouthful of blood. I took one more step and then I vomited. That was worse than the beating. It hurt like hell and my throat burned. I dropped to my knees and kept heaving. It came out of my nose. My ribs were screaming.

When the spasms finally subsided, for some strange reason, the first thing I thought of was Dr. Lewin telling me about the opportunity of rising and rebuilding from the ashes of demolition. I smiled and decided to give it another go at getting up. This time, the ground was more solid beneath my feet. That's when I noticed my feet. They took my shoes and socks. They fucking took my shoes and socks. Then I checked my pockets. They took my wallet. Fuck. No. Wait. I didn't bring my wallet. I brought two cents. I checked my right front pocket. They took the two cents. I smiled. Helluva haul, boys. That was quite a night's work. Hope there's only two of you. Otherwise, the divvying up could get a little tricky.

Despite the pain, I walked home. I must have been a sight. Soaked to the bone, bloody face, and no shoes or socks. There weren't many people on Van Ness, but they avoided me like the homeless. I can't say I blame them. I'm not sure I would have stopped to help me, either.

Walking upstairs to the apartment was difficult. Getting undressed was excruciating. Pissing blood was frightening.

My roommate isn't here. I don't know where he is. He didn't want to stick around after I told him Cynthia's visit might get ugly. He didn't want to hear us argue or make up. He's heard enough of both.

I took some aspirin and sat down to write.

What am I doing? I need to call someone now.

Connie and Jessica

I'm very lucky. I got two broken ribs, a concussion, and various bumps and bruises. But everyone, including all my friends and the police officers that took my statement, are unanimous in their opinion that it could have been much worse. Apparently, I'm not the only person that has been mugged and robbed recently in the Marina district. Some of the victims are still in the hospital. One of them was able to identify three assailants.

That's respectable. There's nothing to be ashamed of when there's three, especially when you don't see them coming and they hit from behind and you're completely defenseless.

Cynthia felt guilty at first, though I made her smile when I wondered how many times in past lives I'd had the crap kicked out of me. She's been very attentive, but my roommate, Roger, Little Tim, and the Castro boys have been unbelievable. They have either made or brought me breakfast and dinner every day since the assault. Roger, Big Tim, and an assortment of large, angry gay men I had never met before have even volunteered to form a little vigilante group once I get well. Roger said the only thing better than revenge was revenge by fags. I giggled, but I think he was serious.

It's been five days since I got stomped and robbed. Today was my first day back at school. It was too much attention but I loved every second. I'm still moving pretty slow, but I've got to get active again. Finals are soon to begin and it's almost time for me to graduate with a Bachelor of Arts in Speech and Communication. It's taken me longer to get my degree than I thought it would when I moved here, but that's the price I've paid for putting myself through college. My parents think I've taken too long, but they respect the fact that I've done it on my own. As soon as I entered the HLL building today, I got hugs and kisses from students and teachers alike. I received intriguing invitations for dinner from two women who heard that Cynthia might be moving.

News certainly does travel fast. I mentioned to Cynthia that at least two women on campus already knew she was leaving. She laughed and shook her head while remarking, "Maybe Connie was right; girls do talk."

I went to the student health center and was examined by Dr. Garza. He remarked that I'd had quite a month or so, in terms of medical incident. He also said that I was due a nice long period of good health.

The best moment by far, however, was when Connie and Jessica spotted me from the quad and then climbed the pyramid steps outside the student union to express their support.

Connie asked, "How the fuck you doing?"

I said, "Better every day. At least I'm not pissing blood anymore."

Jessica smirked. "Oh yeah? Well I am."

Connie grimaced and asked, "You're on the rag?"

Jessica smiled.

Connie said, "Fuck me."

Jessica said, "Not tonight, baby."

"Wait a minute," I asked. "When did you two become a couple?"

Connie answered, "The same night you got stomped."

"Congratulations."

Jessica said proudly, "Thanks."

Connie said, "I hear there were three of them. That's respectable."

I nodded.

There was a pause and then Connie said, "Well, we gotta go."

Then they both leaned over and kissed me on the cheeks.

Jessica added, "Fucking assholes."

Work in the Eighties Part 2

I took the elevator to the fourth floor of Crocker Bank's main branch in San Francisco. The receptionist greeted me with a practiced smile and asked, "May I help you?"

I returned her smile and replied, "Yes, I'm here from the temp agency."

She looked surprised and inquired, "You're the temporary help?"

I nodded and she looked me over even as she answered the phone, "Crocker Bank, may I help you? Yes she is, let me transfer you."

She maintained her quizzical expression and stated, "I thought you were an attorney or something."

I continued smiling and nodding while thinking, *And if I were, would you blow me later*? But I finally offered, "Yes, well, the agency only sends the best."

She stood up and directed, "I should say so. Please follow me."

I did as I was told and caught the eyes of several employees as we proceeded down a long, plush hallway. I stood tall and held my air of professionalism. If anyone else in that office wanted to mistake me for an attorney, up-and-coming entrepreneur, or some other profession of prestige, that was fine with me. After all, I was a recent college graduate with some intriguing credentials and I was wearing my best suit. I did not know what I'd be doing for Crocker, but it had to be better than my previous temporary assignment.

That had been in the mailroom of a large law firm with four other guys. The highlight of any given day had been listening to two of them talk about what they'd like to do to a certain female attorney, while the other two described in minutiae what they'd do with any of about five male attorneys. One day, while seeking refuge in the sanctuary of the men's room, I listened to the same duo expound on what they'd like to do to me.

The receptionist turned into a room and announced, "This will be your office."

Well oh my, I thought, but said, "Yes, thank you, this will do nicely."

"Oh, I'm sure it will," she slyly responded, then continued. "Your supervisor will be here shortly." She moved out the door and added, "Have a nice day."

She disappeared from view, but I said after her, "Thank you again. I'll see you later."

I turned and went to the window behind my desk and gazed down on the daily madness of the financial district. *Yes, this is where a man belongs*, I thought as I watched a messenger cyclist narrowly avoid being run over by a Jaguar. I scanned the buildings across the street, wondering what else I could see from my office. That is to say, My Office. Directly across from me on Market Street, I noticed a young woman sitting by a window at her desk and she seemed to be looking at me. She had nice legs. I smiled and slightly nodded my head. To my surprise, she smiled and waved her left hand. She did not seem to be wearing a ring. *Nice legs and no ring*, I thought and warmly returned her wave with my own left hand sans ring, quickly thinking of something clever to do, or how I might signal her to meet me for lunch.

"Mr. Morehead?"

I turned suddenly and saw another woman at the door.

"Mr. Morehead, I'm Ms. Munshaw, how do you do?"

I recovered from my surprise and accepted her extended hand.

"A pleasure to meet you, Ms. Munshaw, and allow me to say right away, I'm impressed with the spacious accommodations," and I gestured around the room.

She smiled with slight surprise and said, "I'm glad you think so. We've found a comfortable environment increases productivity."

I agreed. "That is so true. Why, when I was in school, I always tried to be as comfortable as possible."

She nodded her head in eager approval and sat down while asking, "When did you graduate?"

I sat down as well, noticing for the first time that both chairs were folding chairs. This momentarily caught me off guard, but I quickly recovered and answered, "Two months ago."

She crossed her right leg over her left and tugged her skirt over her knee while asking, "So what career do you intend to pursue?"

I looked at her earnestly and replied, "Well, I'm still looking, exploring all my options. But to be honest, I like what I see here."

Ms. Munshaw nodded and barely smiled as if she expected someone as bright and intelligent and well dressed as I was to answer that way. She advised, "Well, we're always on the lookout for sharp young talent. You can't get enough bright people willing to start at the bottom and work their way up."

I nodded back at her and smiled, all the while wondering how low the bottom was going to be there. She uncrossed her legs and leaned forward on her chair.

"So as you know," she began, "we've contracted you from the agency for a rather monumental task."

Though I'd been told nothing about the assignment other than where to report and to dress well, I thought, *Yes indeed, this is more like it*, and my nodding gained momentum.

"We want you to stuff, lick, and stamp ten thousand envelopes."

My nodding slowed to a crawl and my face sagged.

Ms. Munshaw immediately looked concerned and asked, "Are you alright?"

I tried to regain a measure of dignity as I admitted, "They didn't tell me what I'd be doing."

She looked shocked and asked, "They didn't? Did they tell you how much you're being paid?"

"No," I answered and finally stopped nodding.

"$4.25 an hour."

Slowly I began nodding again while noticing the stacks of boxes lining the wall behind Ms. Munshaw.

Her smile returned while confidently asking, "You're going to do it of course, aren't you?"

"Of course," I replied.

Ms. Munshaw stood up and started for the door while enthusiastically saying, "Great! All the supplies are right here and feel free to help yourself to some coffee. If you have any questions, I'll be in the office to your immediate left."

She paused by the door and added, "Oh and one other thing. You should probably get several glasses of water. Licking is tiring work. And watch out for paper cuts."

I Wish I Brought a Camera

I decided not to work this week. I turned down an assignment because I had enough money saved from various temporary jobs to survive for a while, or move away, and I needed to make a decision. Was I going to stay or was I going to go? It's what everyone wanted to know, myself included. With each day of delay, the choice had become more complicated. Cynthia seems either happy and inspired, or completely brainwashed in El Cajon. She even sounds genuine when she says she misses me and hopes I make the move. I'm also tempted to stick around San Francisco for Gwen's return to the Bay Area. On top of that, Stephanie, the receptionist from the temporary job I had at Crocker Bank, has been a warm and welcome diversion. She has a body like Patti D'Arbanville in that film *Bilitis,* and she reminds me of my old friend Maureen, because she expects nothing more from me than good company and the occasional sharing of intimacy. But all these things have only led me to a greater degree of confusion.

So I asked my roommate for a large favor and because he is who he is, he let me borrow his '72 Chevy Malibu for a solo outing to The Sea. If I told him I was going any other place, he probably would have said no. But it was a request he could not turn down. I'd introduced him to The Sea, just like I had almost every other close friend of mine since the spring of 1978, when I chanced upon it by pure necessity and it marked me forever.

Though it was only January, the winter rains of northern California had already turned the coastal hills that glimmering, almost fluorescent green, reminding everyone that even the earth cannot wait for spring. It was a crystal clear day, surprisingly in the mid-sixties, and miraculously without much wind as the Malibu and I rolled down the coast highway. I cued up one of the cassettes I brought, featuring *Incantations* by Mike Oldfield, and then filled in at the end with "Spider and I" by Brian Eno and, finally, the tribal Sea song, "On Presuming to be Modern," by Synergy. As I drove, I vacillated somewhere between serious internal debate and an almost overwhelming nostalgia. I'd been on that road so many times, with so many friends, and in such varied states of consciousness. Back in the days I had a car, before I totaled it and almost killed two friends, and myself, I made that drive as often as some people go to church. In fact, the comparison is apt, because going to The Sea is like going to church for me, just as it is for some of the friends I've taken there. I rolled down the driver's side window, turned up the music, and ran my left hand through my hair, ruefully noting how much of it I removed with the simple gesture. It blew off my fingers, out the window, and into memory as quickly, it seemed, as the passing of my youth.

Despite this rather depressing, relatively new reality, I was excited at the prospect of the day. In all the years I'd been making this trek, I'd never gone by myself. I had always gone to The Sea with someone, and every single time I went, all those people seemed to be with me again. I was convinced the very place, and probably the process itself, retained memory.

So I was surprised and a little bothered when I pulled off the road and found another car parked in the narrow and barely long enough piece of dirt reserved for only those who know. I didn't want to be with anyone or be seen by anyone. I wanted the place all to myself. I briefly considered driving on and looking for another spot. But there is no other spot, and I knew it. I grabbed my thermos of ice tea, locked up the car, and started looking for the trail. It didn't take long.

Once heading down the narrow cliff toward the jagged rocks, with the cove to my left and The Sea getting closer with each step, I felt better. I stopped briefly to look, breathe it in, and let it take over. Man, how could someone else being there possibly bother me? In addition to everything on my mind, I needed to work on that.

At the narrowest point of the trail, I looked to my left, down and into the cove, where water and kelp continually come and go, sometimes crashing, sometimes sliding and spreading up to the small, sandy beach, depending on whether the tide is high or low. I only climbed down there once and would never do so again. It was a beautiful cove to look at, but it would be a miserable place to die, and the night I spent there with a group was fun, but potentially perilous and flat out cold.

I continued down the trail, past ice plant and what I knew were the beginnings of iris, Indian paintbrush, and lupine. My steps were as sure as collective memory, though always aware that a wrong move to my right or left could bring pain and disaster, if not mortality. Yet, my mind and soul were unburdened and I knew that if I did die there, that day or any other day, the place would make good use of me and I would be assured of as much private time as I could imagine.

I found a spot to maneuver and drop over jagged rocks in order to reach the surface of what only extreme high tide disallowed to remain relatively dry. There was a protected beach of rocks, and the miraculous sitting pool, into which many of my closest friends and I have sat naked and pondering. Because the area is partially blocked from the westerly flow of air and actually slightly below the surface of the ocean, the air temperature is always warmer during the day and colder at night.

I stood by the pool and looked at my reflection. In that pristine water, I saw the faces of friends and some who used to be friends. They had all been road companions at one time or another and each of them had all gazed into the pool. There were also a few faces I did not know, but I presumed they chanced upon this place in similar fashion to me. Looking into that pool is as close as I've ever come to an acid flashback, shared moment, or waking dream.

Then I glanced up from the water and saw what I always saw when I looked due north from that spot. It stood as it always stood, firm and erect. But it wasn't time to acknowledge it by name just yet. There was a proper sequence of events that had to take place and this was merely the end of the first of those moments.

I turned west and climbed about ten feet of jagged, pocked rock, sunburnt to a crisp orange and brown. A small amount of mussels clung to those rocks, but as long as they stayed there, they were doomed and they knew it. They could only hope for a tide so strong as to remove them from their dwindling grip and carry them to a new foothold, or return them to the deep.

At that point, each step brought me closer to the main reason I came. With each intake, I felt the air go deeper into my lungs, and with each exhale, I felt clarity rising closer to the surface. I was exactly where I needed to be. I was, once again, at The Sea.

And I was not alone.

About twenty-five feet to my left and south, on a small slab of rock below a much larger peak covered with ice plant, sat an old man. He had to be at least eighty, with a nose that at first glance seemed crooked, a mostly bald head, a silver gray beard, and slightly over-sized, horn-rimmed glasses. He looked frail against the backdrop of dramatic green hills, treacherously slippery kelp-covered rocks, moss and tide pools that endured almost relentless, torrential pounding ocean. I couldn't believe a man that elderly had made the same hike and descent as I.

He turned slightly in my direction and then did a startled double take when he saw me. He smiled slightly while shaking his head, waved his arm in greeting, and said, "Hello young man, you gave me a start. How long you been there?"

"I just got here."

His smile broadened as he said, "Well, welcome to you. It seems at least two minds have thought alike today. What brings you here?"

There was absolutely no reason to answer his question with anything other than the truth. I said, "I've got some things on my mind to sort out and this is my favorite place on earth."

He nodded and added, "It's a great place, that's for sure. It isn't my favorite place, but it's not far behind. What's your name?"

"Dave. And yours?"

"My name . . ." and just then, a huge wave crashed against the first bank of rocks bordering the ocean no more than fifty feet in front of the old man. He quickly turned to see how far the water would advance, so either he did not tell me his name, or I did not hear it. I thought about asking again, but it didn't seem important and I figured the only proper thing to call him was sir.

"It's a pleasure to meet you, sir."

He quickly assessed he was in no danger of being swept from the rocks, turned toward me again, and said, "The pleasure is all mine, Dave. Why don't you park yourself next to me on this convenient piece of evolutionary masonry and take a load off?"

His invitation was as impossible to resist as his smile, which featured a pretty full set of dentures. There was something familiar about him, like I should know him. But mostly he struck me as impish, elfish, and really cute. His eyes, though squinted from sunlight and glare off the water, positively sparkled with the possibility of mirth. He certainly was no curmudgeon, at least not that day.

I climbed to the ledge, the very spot I had intended to sit, and a place I spent in considerable reflection almost every time I'd been there. It wasn't just the conveniently located ledge and the relatively safe distance it afforded between yourself and the roiling water. It was also a spot with a full panorama. From there, you could look north, south, or west and feel surrounded by the vast Pacific, yet still with enough rocks, pools, and blow holes to offer some protection against sneaker waves. There were also escape routes to higher ground if you saw a big one coming, as well as a firm slab of rock immediately behind, to grab and hold on against an engulfing wave and its retreating tide. At least, that had always been my opinion, as well as the consensus of others through the years that risked all by sitting there. Further, this strategy had proven itself, replete with legendary tales of full-body drenching, near catastrophe, and genuine, though foolish bravery. This was also one of the most dramatic and purely romantic destinations I'd ever been. I kissed several women there. I fantasized that someday, on that very spot, I would propose to the love of my life.

I sat next to the elderly man and placed my notebook between us on the rock, with thermos on top, so the book would not get blown open or away should a sudden gust arrive. I felt compelled to share with him what I knew about the spot and the various safety strategies. But I had to know something first.

I asked, "Please excuse me sir, for asking you this, but isn't the hike down here a little perilous for a man your age?"

He looked at me sharply and asked, "Do I look feeble?"

"No sir, you do not," I answered immediately and was mortified that I'd opened my mouth and implied such a presumption. I quickly added, "But the trail gets so narrow and there is some descent involved and . . ." I hesitated, suddenly aware of my shoe tickling my uvula.

He finished my thought, "And I'm an old fart who couldn't possibly get down here on his own."

"I apologize, sir. I did not mean to insult you. Sometimes, I still speak before I think."

"That's okay, you're a young man. I was the same way at your age. You probably still think you're immortal."

He turned and took me in with an assessment stare and then revised, "Well, maybe not. I can see a little curl at your edges."

What a little wise guy, I thought, though I could not stop from broadly smiling at his description of me.

He continued, "Okay then, if you don't mind me asking, and I don't know why you would, since our time to share a moment of life is probably confined to right now, exactly what brings you here?"

I answered, "Should I stay or should I go?"

He guessed, "A woman?"

I nodded.

"Do you love her?"

"Yes, but I'm not in love with her anymore, if you know what I mean."

He stared at the sea before answering, "I know exactly what you mean."

Of course, my situation was a little more complicated than that, so I added, "The thing is, her family, her friends, the people that have known her longest, they've all pretty much given up on her."

He looked at me again and said, "So she's got some sort of problem then."

I agreed and added, "Yes, she does, but she hasn't realized it yet, and I'm the only one that's stayed by to remind her."

He commiserated, "That's a pretty big burden."

I nodded again.

We let the sounds around us take over for a few minutes as he pondered the wisdom or folly of me following my instincts.

Eventually, he changed the subject by asking, "What did you bring in that thermos?"

"Ice tea."

He nodded and said, "That's a good choice, though I wish you had something in there a little stronger."

"I don't do that and then drive. I used to, but I almost killed some people once, on that very road up there."

He offered, "You know what I think you should do?"

I couldn't resist. "You think I should drive into town, and pick up some Metamucil that we could mix into the tea."

The burst of laughter almost sent his teeth onto the rocks, but he caught them before they fully emerged and shoved them back into place even as he rocked back and forth with giggles.

"Nice catch," I added.

"Thank you," he acknowledged, while turning and fully taking me into his sight.

I was cognizant he was staring at me, but there was something about it that was not invasive. In fact, it almost felt as if he had withdrawn from me and was looking at me from a distance. Finally, he said, "I wish I brought a camera. Someone should photograph that beard of yours. It's a beauty."

The remark caught me by surprise. I'd been growing my beard since around Thanksgiving the previous year. I'd never done it before and it was fun. I called it my hippie phase. Cynthia told me that she missed my face and I said that she'd miss it even more after she moved. Roger said all I needed was overalls and then I could begin my career as a muleskinner.

"Thank you, sir. I appreciate that. I like it, too."

After a few more moments of silence, he said, "I think you already know what you're going to do. You'd just like someone to give you permission."

"Are you that someone?"

"No."

"It's all on me, isn't it?"

"Yes," he agreed, but then added, "I will say this, though. I give you permission to do what you know is right, even if no one else agrees. Because at the end of the day, you don't have to answer to them."

I let his words enter me and move around. I allowed them to join the sea air with all those wonderful negative ions, and I knew my decision had just been reached. Whatever lay ahead, in that moment I felt the easing of a burden.

I suddenly proclaimed, "I like the word serendipity."

Without a hitch, he agreed, "So do I. Always have."

I added, "It feels like that today."

He nodded, and then replied, "But sometimes, people think that word is something lucky or coincidental. Of course, it can be. It's happened to me. And I agree it feels that way today. But the best moments of serendipity I've ever known were a product of planning and vision, much more than chance."

It sounded like invaluable advice, but I didn't exactly understand him.

He saw my look of confusion and added, "What I mean, and you might still be too young to understand this, but if you can, you need to envision your future, see it as clearly as possible, and as what you want it to be, before you can know the steps you need to take to make it happen."

I nodded my head appreciatively toward him, immediately aware those words needed to be pondered and would probably live inside me the rest of my life. But at that moment, I knew exactly what was in my future.

I said, "Right now, I envision a urination of Biblical proportions, and the steps I need to take are over there by that wading pool, against the wall that borders the rock beach and shields any visibility from the road."

He giggled and as I rose, he said, "Ah yes, the tribal pissing grounds. That's the same spot I use."

I stopped and asked, "You call it the tribal pissing grounds, too? That's what a friend of mine and I have always called it."

He nodded, "Clearly, it's another example of great minds thinking alike."

I said, "Wait just a minute, then come over there and join me. There's something I want to show you."

He got up, pretty damn spry, I must add, and said, "Why wait? We might as well make a pilgrimage. That's sort of what my life is about these days, anyway."

So we walked, both of us careful and mindful the ocean was at our back, until descending into the tribal pissing ground. We handled our business and then I directed him to look in the distance, past the wading pool, toward more rocks and small cliffs, simultaneously similar and yet remarkably different in countless ways. I asked him if he saw anything unusual, and then I hinted to look for something remarkably familiar to both of us, cut, worn, and hone through time by ocean, sun, and wind.

He seemed to delight in this. As I watched him trying to spot the answer to the riddle, it occurred to me that given his vast experience, and how sharp his mind still was, he was probably taking in more information than I was capable. It seemed to me that he could see things, shapes and shadows, perhaps even portents that I could not as yet grasp.

But I still had something on him, and it was driving him a little crazy. He put his hands on his hips and looked like he was about to speak several times before thinking better of it and shaking his head. It was a perfect moment, and I didn't want to ruin it, but I felt compelled to needle him just a bit by asking, "You give?"

"You're rotten," he half scolded. "Just give me a minute. I'm seeing too much. I need to think about what you'd see in all that."

That was a curious response, almost patronizing, and I could tell by the direction of his eyes, he was close.

"There It Is!" he proclaimed, pointing a finger excitedly. "Oh boy, there it is. I've looked over there a hundred times at least and never seen it. But it's as plain as it can be."

Of course, what he had seen and what he was describing was the end of a large rock structure about thirty yards in the distance that my friend Rod and I had come to simply call the Cock. Chiseled and lubricated by the ocean over a period of time incalculable, that's what it looked like, an erect and fully engorged penis.

He said, "That's quite a cock, no question about it. Why did you show it to me?"

"Because one of the things I've always done here, before I, or anyone I'm with, can leave, is to hit that cock with one of these stones by our feet. We have to throw it from here and hit it."

His face sagged and he admitted, "I don't have the arm for that anymore."

I felt noble as I offered, "With your permission then, I will take the turn for both of us. You, however, must pick out your own stone for the throw."

"You got a deal," he responded and went to his task.

Within a few minutes, we had each picked three, though I made it clear that we might have to pick more. I told him it had taken me as many as twenty to thirty attempts, or as few as two, to hit the Cock.

He said, "Well then, I'm just going to stand back here and root you on. Try not to break it, though. Now that I've seen it, it would be a shame not to find it here again."

I nodded, but cautioned, "I'll do the best I can, but I can't make any promises. It's a risky business, throwing rocks at a cock."

"But noble sport," he acknowledged.

"Indeed, sir. Shall I commence?"

"Yes, sir," he said, offering me one of his stones and presuming that his turn should be first.

"Age before beauty," I commented, thinking it a clever needle.

"Without question," he volleyed with precision. "This stone is far older than I."

I nodded, turned, took aim, and made a direct strike at the base of the shaft, causing a slight change in color for the spot where the stone struck.

"Well done!" he shouted. "Look how you bruised the brute."

I was pleased. I'd never before hit the Cock on a first shot.

"Now take your own turn," he advised. "But you have to hit it on your first shot as well, or I'm the winner."

I remarked, "You have gotten into the spirit of this game, haven't you?"

It took me three shots before striking a glancing blow on the top that sent a scattering of scrapings and sea dust into the air. I turned, walked to the man and offered my hand, saying, "Congratulations, sir. Clearly you are the champion of the day. You have successfully allowed me to beat myself at my own game, an accomplishment that is as pleasing as it is humbling."

"And best of all," he advised, "the Cock remains."

"As it should," I concurred before adding, "I suggest you keep your remaining stones as souvenirs. Perhaps you'll bring them with you the next time you come here."

On that seemingly hopeful note, he looked a little sad, though he nodded his head. Instead, he gently placed the stones back on the ground and began to return to our sitting spot. I followed him and when we were seated again, I opened the thermos and filled the top with tea. I offered it to him and he drank the full cup. After I had my fill, we sat in silence and watched the water.

Finally, he said, "I won't be back here again. I can't imagine a better way to say good-bye to this place than this."

I think I understood, but I felt obliged to encourage at least some discussion. I asked, "How can you be so sure?"

He continued looking at the water while saying, "Because that's what this year is all about for me. Going to the places I love and saying good-bye while I still can." He seemed to realize this news was rather a downer after all the joy that preceded it. So he was quick to add, "Don't misunderstand. I've still got a lot of places to go before I'm through. The end won't be for quite some time and when it comes, I'll be kicking and screaming."

I said, "Just make sure you keep one hand free to hold those teeth in place."

He snorted, shook his head, and turned to me, smiling. He was about to say something caustic, I could tell, something that would have completely put me in my place. But instead, his eyes suddenly widened and he shouted, "Look At That!"

I turned to my left to share his vision, but all I saw was the epic coastline, coves, water, the two large rocks about a mile out in the ocean that always served as landmarks for my arrival, and the long, sloping green hill in the southernmost distance, the end of which gave way to a tiny shell beach that I wish I could have shown this man. I saw all these things, just as I had so many times before, and yet I knew this was not what he had seen. I glanced back at him and asked, "What was it?"

He shook his head and said, "Something I've seen here before."

"What was it?" I pressed.

He barely smiled, slightly sighed, and said, "It was just a moment, impossible to describe. It was a feeling, really, and now it's gone."

Suddenly, I realized I needed to leave. The Sea has been my place of refuge and source of inspiration since I was in the infancy of my manhood. It will always be my most special place. But at that moment, realizing why the old man was there, I had to go. I had my time with him and I did not want to further intrude, or wear out my welcome.

I knew I'd be back someday. In fact, I could see it. I could envision it. I would take the steps to make it so. I don't yet know what those steps will be, but I know the next time I come to The Sea, I will be with my true love. She's out there and she's waiting for me. I felt such gratitude to this great, old man and our chance encounter. I wanted to thank him. I even thought about reading him the poem I'd been working on called The Sea. But I didn't. The poem isn't finished yet, and neither am I.

I said, "I need to go now, sir. I've got a long drive home and a lot to do before the things that come next."

He nodded his head and said, "I understand. Good luck, young man. Today has been an unexpected treat."

I put the top back on the thermos, screwed on the cup, picked up my notebook and offered my hand. He shook it and we said good-bye. I briefly considered offering to help him up the trail, but I knew that was unnecessary. The old man had clearly hiked far more difficult trails than the one leading to the road from The Sea.

Thank You

This one hurts. This is my last journal entry, for now, from San Francisco, in the bedroom of the apartment where I've been living for four years. Tomorrow morning, I will throw the last boxes and bags into the back of the U-Haul and drive to El Cajon.

The reason I'm writing this and the reason I'm going to rip it from the book and post it on the fridge is for you.

Yes, you. My roommate. You are the man who has been and shall remain nameless, because that's what you wanted and I'm a man of my word.

That said, I have to write this. That's why I'm leaving it on the fridge. But don't put it past me to make a copy. You know how anal I am about the words.

You have been a fine roommate. You will always be a friend, but our time of sharing a living space has come to an end.

Thank you for all you have done during these years. Thank you for all the talks, meals, occasional fronting of rent or phone bill money. Thank you for being honest with me and calling me on my bullshit. Thank you for growing with me. We both used to be pretty bad, regarding the shapes of some and the lifestyles of others, but we're okay now. Thank you for listening to my music and for some of the music you brought into my life. I give you permission to start listening to reggae again, even though I have no respect for that music and all the hypocrisy of peace, love, smoke ganja, Rastafarians yeah, we're all brothers and sisters, except we FUCKING HATE FAGGOTS.

Smoka da dope.
Sit in da chair
Stay dere too long
Won't go anywhere

Thank you for clearing out when private time was required. Thank you for helping me clean before my parents visited. Thank you for listening to me rant on and on about my problems. I hope I was as good a listener for you. Thank you for letting me read, ad nauseam, from my journals and thank you for insisting I listen to you read from yours. Thank you for letting old friends of mine visit for days on end and play music best suited for cats in heat. Thank you for helping me throw a couple of them out. Thank you for not becoming an EST hole, like some of your former friends. Thank you for introducing me to the miracle of Corticaine Cream and sharing yours. I'll never do cocaine, since I've done Corticaine.

Thank you for understanding, even if you don't agree, why I have to go now.

I know we'll keep in touch, but please keep me posted of any important news or rumors. Just because we're at opposite ends of the state, doesn't mean we have to stop gossiping.

And please let me know if you get any further news on Little Tim. If it's that gay cancer thing, call me immediately. WAKE ME UP! I hate leaving Roger right now.

So this is it for the time being, roomie. Your secrets and your name shall go with me. By the way, you're snoring right now, ya fuck.

See you —Dave

PS. The new roommate told me he couldn't wait to shower with you. He was so excited.

Work in the Eighties Part 3

"You'll be paid the minimum wage plus commissions and I'm tellin' ya', this is a great bidness to start young. So if you don't have any more questions, let's go out and rustle us some customers. Oh, and by the way, everyone around here calls me SH."

"Let's get 'em, SH," I said, and so began my career selling cars in El Cajon, California.

It was 102 degrees and the other salesmen were in short-sleeved shirts and clip-on ties. I didn't dare remove my wool sports jacket, lest everyone think I'd just poured water under my arms and down my back clear to my ass crack. SH described our dealership as "A good ol' country lot" and a "Friendly, down-home sorta place." He also explained that ours was a "Turnover lot." That meant once you had a customer and had maybe taken them for a test drive, you would then "turn the deal over" to another salesman. That man would always be introduced as your sales manager, and then he would attempt to close the deal.

We walked toward the far end of the lot, where a middle-aged couple was eyeing a white, 1979 Hondamatic. SH instructed, "Let me do the talkin', Dave, and I'll teach ya' the ABCs."

The couple turned toward us as they saw us approach and SH hailed them, "Hey hey, how you folks doin' on a day as fine as this?"

"Chuch chichn," the man answered and I immediately knew he'd had a tracheotomy, because he was speaking out of a hole in his throat.

"What he say?" SH asked cheerfully.

"He said just fine," replied the woman.

SH shook their hands and said, "Real good. Now listen, my name's Steve and this here is Dave Morehead. He just started with us."

I said, "A pleasure," as I shook hands with both of them.

"Cochachuachonch, chere Chanch chan Chonnich," the man said.

SH patted him joyfully on the back and inquired, "What he say?"

The woman answered, "He said congratulations, we're Frank and Bonnie."

SH exploded, "Well real good, Frank and Bonnie. I see you all are interested in our lil' ol' Hondamatic."

Bonnie said, "Well, we're just looking."

SH looked like the happiest man on earth and his volume raised a notch. "Well of course you are, and you all've come to the right place to look!"

Frank nodded toward Bonnie and said, "Chach's chwach Chi cholch chou."

SH grabbed Frank behind the neck and smiled while asking, "What did this ol' rascal just say?"

Bonnie forced a smile and answered, "He said, that's what I told you."

SH clapped Frank hard on the shoulder and bellowed, "See? See right there? I told you, why, I tell ya'."

Frank immediately produced a cough that sounded like a bag being emptied of nickels and dimes.

"Is he alright?" SH asked.

"He's fine," Bonnie replied, "as long as you don't break his back."

SH ignored the admonition and continued, "Well, I'll just bet he's fine. Any man with his kinda sense is fine in my book, I'll tell ya'. So how would you folks like to take this little baby for a spin?"

Frank wiped his throat with a handkerchief and said, "Chanch chon'ch che chechechery."

"How's that?" SH asked.

Bonnie answered, "He says that won't be necessary."

SH recoiled and pretended to slam his hand against his forehead while saying, "No test drive? Are you sure?"

Frank replied, "Chesch."

SH rolled his eyes deliriously toward the sky and then back to the couple while he proclaimed, "Well Lordy, I'll be a son of a gun. What have we got here? Have we got us a real wheeler dealer?"

Frank smiled and nodded.

SH walked over and put his ham hock arm around my shoulders, asking, "Are you payin' attention to this, Dave? We mighta met our match with this ol' boy."

SH kept the hock around me and cooed, "Well folks, I got an idea. It's pretty doggone hot out here. Why don't we all go inside where's it's shady and talk us some turkey?"

They agreed and we started toward the showroom. SH and I led the way and as we walked ahead, he told me, "This is where you would ordinarily turn the deal over to someone else, but seein' how I'm trainin' ya', I'll just do the whole shebang."

"No problem, boss," I agreed while thinking this was the most entertained I'd been since moving from San Francisco to this hellish shit hole in the desert near the Mexican border for a woman and relationship that could only end soon.

He rested his arm around me again and leaned close while whispering, "Mind ya', not all the fuckers are as easy as this ol' boy. But pay attention anyway, 'cause the next hour or so's the fun part."

"Go get 'em, SH," I said.

He clapped me on the shoulder and intoned, "That's m'boy. Go get 'em."

We walked into the showroom and waited for Frank and Bonnie to catch up. As they entered, SH turned toward Stan, another salesman I'd met earlier, who was reading the sports section of the San Diego Union, and roared, "Mr. Stan-Lee, I'll tell ya', I got me a shrewd son of a buck right here," while gesturing toward Frank.

Stan casually said, "A tough nut, huh?" and he glanced at Frank, who was smiling. Stan returned to his sports page, only to then perform a classic double take at Frank and the gaping hole in his throat.

"Chi chachnch chornch checherchach," Frank stated with pride.

"Huh?" asked Stan.

"He said, I wasn't born yesterday," I said to Stan while Bonnie gave me a sincere look of thanks.

"I should think not," acknowledged Stan, by then resuming a preview about the San Diego Padres for the upcoming baseball season.

"Well here we are," SH announced and motioned everyone into an office down a short hallway.

"Just sit yourselves down here in the shade," SH cooed, "while Dave and I get ya' each a glass full o' ice cold water."

"Chanch chouch," said Frank as they sat down.

"Did he just say thank you?" asked SH.

When Bonnie nodded, SH just shook his head and proclaimed, "Well, isn't that somethin'? You are somethin' an' then some!"

I closed the door and followed SH the remainder of the hall to his office. He handed me two paper cups and pointed toward an adjacent bathroom. I opened the door, walked in, and looked around for a refrigerator or some kind of water cooler. Seeing nothing but a toilet, sink, and mirror, I turned to SH and asked, "Where's the cold water?"

SH looked at me and furrowed his almost unibrow while saying, "Son, where there's a sink, there's cold water. Din't they teach you that in school?"

He caught my look of surprise and continued, "Look here, if those folks look at ya' kinda funny when ya' hand 'em a cup of lukewarm water, just tell 'em the ice machine broke down. Now go on an' give 'em that water an' then come on back here. I wanna talk with you."

I took Frank and Bonnie their water and the first thing I noticed when I entered the room was the extreme heat. It was significantly warmer in the room than it had been outside.

"Thank you," Bonnie said while I leaned across the table where they were seated and attempted to open the window. It would not budge.

"Che chachechy chniech chich," Frank said.

I asked, "You did?"

Bonnie said, "Yes."

"Well follow me," I instructed. "Let's get you into another office."

We went across the hall into an almost identical room that was about the same temperature. The window would not open there, either.

SH suddenly appeared in the doorway and said, "Well now, don't tell me you tried to open the windows."

"They won't open," I replied with frustration.

SH walked to the window and ran his fingers softly over the mostly filthy glass. He turned around with sorrowful eyes and shook his head while saying, "Well, I guess this is jus' the price we pay in America for vandalism."

"Vandalism!" cried Bonnie.

SH turned quickly and looked out the window, as if it was hard to talk, or perhaps he was just longing for better times from days gone by. Somehow from those deep emotions, he found it within himself to try and explain.

SH said, "Yes'm, you folks mighta even read or heard about this a couple months back. It made page four of the local. But there was this group o' damn Mexicans, pardon my language ma'm, they were from the other side of the border, and they tried to bomb us."

"BOMB YOU?" wailed Bonnie.

"Yes'm," confirmed SH as he clenched his right fist and shook it gently at the window. He continued, "Why I tell you, I wish I'd a caught 'em before the police came."

Bonnie relaxed slightly and asked, "Was anyone hurt?"

SH turned and faced them again. He lowered his voice and unclenched his fist while saying, "No ma'm, but ever since then, we jus' felt the windows should be closed at all times."

"Chy chid chey chy choo chom chou?"

"Yeah, I was wondering the same thing," I added.

SH fixed a confused and frustrated look at me as Bonnie said, "He wants to know why they wanted to bomb you."

SH looked angry, but he maintained his composure. "Bonnie, Frank, I wish I could tell ya'. They got away before anythin' could blow up or they got caught. Someone in the garage said somethin' about one of our mechanics and someone's sister, but it's hard to know for sure. I don't speak the language. We got rid of the mechanic, but we're keepin' the windows shut awhile longer, jus' t' be safe."

"Chey choucha chok chech, Choch chamich!" Frank angrily stated.

Bonnie looked at her husband with shock and disappointment and softly scolded, "Franklin, please don't use the Lord's name in vain."

Frank nodded his apologies to all of us while SH headed for the door, saying, "As I say, one of these days, we'll have 'em fixed, but I'll tell ya' what. Why don't ya' jus' sit right down and sip on soma that cool water. Dave an' I will be right back." Again, SH closed the door.

We got to his office and SH sat down. He propped his boots on his desk before saying, "Dave, grab a chair."

I sat down, and then SH said, "Now son, I can tell you're a good boy an' you're bright, an' that's why I hired ya'. But I can tell I'm gonna haf' t' teach ya' 'bout the real world."

He got up and walked into the bathroom, where he faced the mirror, splashed some Vitalis into his hands and began rubbing them through his thick, wavy, and already completely Vitalisised hair. He started combing it and said, "Jus' so ya' know it, there weren't no vandals. The windows are supposed to be closed. They won't ever open. Those offices are called sweat boxes, on account o' we want people t' sweat in there."

"There were no Mexicans?" was all I could think to ask.

"Hell no, boy," he flatly stated while clapping me on the shoulder on the way back to his seat. My jacket instantly began saturating Vitalis. The stench and stain would only increase each day I spent on that lot.

As he sat down, he laughed and continued, "'Course, that ain't true. There's more Mexicans around here than Americans. But if I saw one o' them over-the-border sons o' bitches near here, I'd kick his ass all-the-way-back-to-Mexicali."

This set him off in a full laugh, clapping his generous stomach as he leaned back in his chair. When his laugh slowed to a chuckle and finally a sigh, I asked, "So aren't we gonna go in there and talk turkey with those people?"

SH fixed a thoughtful gaze at me for a few moments before asking, "What city did you say you wuz from?"

"San Francisco."

SH immediately nodded his head as if that was the answer. He advised, "Son, you've got to understand somethin'. Down here, you're dealin' with a man's world. You've got t' learn how to deal with real people. You been up there with those faggots, so you kinda forgot what the real world is like."

He paused and looked at me squarely before asking, "You did say you got a girlfriend, right? What's she like?"

I smiled and answered truthfully, "She believes in reincarnation and life on other planets."

SH stared at me hard, but his face quickly gave way to a smile and he said, "Like I said, I hired ya' 'cause you're a bright boy an' I think yer gonna do fine in this bidness. But just for today, I don't want you to say another word."

I said, "So for today, SH stands for shh."

His smile broadened while he said, "Ab-so-lutely. I think you'll learn more by jus' lis'nen."

SH got up and announced, "Gotta pinch one. When I'm done, we'll go back in there."

It was twenty minutes later before we checked in on Frank and Bonnie. When we opened the door, the density of the heat caused my eyes to slightly water in both protest and protection. Frank was swabbing the hole in his throat and both their cups were empty.

We sat down across from them and SH earnestly said, "Sorry for the delay, folks. I mighta told ya' already, but this is Dave here's first day an' I had t' explain the paperwork."

Before Frank or Bonnie could say anything, SH slapped a purchase agreement on the table and proclaimed, "Well, Dave 'n me talked about it long 'n hard, and we think this is the price you're lookin' for."

On the bottom of the document, SH had written a price $100 more than the price written on the car.

Bonnie noticed this first and asked SH, "Why is this more than the sticker price?"

SH nodded and said, "That's because the sticker price is before we do one last complete maintenance and inspection, which we do for 50 percent off the normal price. It's jus' one o' the services we do t' keep our customers happy."

Bonnie nodded slightly, but didn't look entirely pleased as she said, "Well, that's awfully nice, but it's still more than we wanted to spend. We're using the remainder of Frank's workers' compensation from his accident at the plant and . . ."

"What kind of accident? What plant?" I interrupted.

SH immediately said, "Dave, why don't you go get us all some water?"

His tone left no doubt I was not to wait for Bonnie to answer and before she could, SH bellowed, "Frank, you sly ol' dog. You been sittin' there sayin' nuthin'. But I know you been thinkin' a mile a minute. Whadaya think 'bout all this?"

Even from the bathroom inside SH's office, I could hear some low, muffled, choking sounds coming from Frank.

Bonnie said, "Frank's throat is all dried out from the heat. I'll have to do the talking."

I heard SH get up and say, "I understand. Listen, I'm gonna see what's keepin' Dave with that water. Why don't you two talk it over and we'll be right back," and he closed the office door as he left.

He entered his own office and closed the door before saying, "Now Dave, I know you wuz jus' tryin' t' show some concern and these are folks who 'preciate that type o' thing. But in cases like this, you got t' use some common sense. That poor ol' fucker's about to die in there. I wanna close 'em an' git 'em the fuck outahere."

Despite this apparent rush, SH sat down at his desk and lit a smoke. After two full drags, he went out to the showroom and retrieved the newspaper Stan had been reading earlier and proclaimed, "This is gonna be the Padres' year."

After several minutes of silent contemplation, I finally said, "You know, SH, I was thinking . . ."

SH held up his hand and ordered, "Dave, don't think. Thinkin' is for the constipated."

He roared with laughter, as did Stan from his next-door office.

SH got up and said, "Come on, boy. I want you t' be as quiet as a mute, 'cept don't do the gruntin' part, an' listen real close at how I close this deal."

We returned to the office and I placed the refilled cups of water on the table. Bonnie grabbed her cup and gulped it down. She was sweating freely and strands of her bangs lay matted on her forehead. Frank had his handkerchief tied around his throat and it was nearly soaked.

Bonnie put down the cup and said, "Frank says to knock off that hundred and you've got a deal. He can work on the car himself."

SH's face burst into appreciation and he blared, "Doggone it all, I shoulda thought o' that. Any real man always know how t' fix his own car. You learnin' somethin' here, boy?" His wreaking hand once more found my shoulder, the other shoulder.

I nodded and said, "You bet."

"Well then," SH concluded, while writing the new figure and circling it. "Jus' sign right here, then go on roun' the corner to accountin', an you can drive it home. It's been a pleasure, folks, and Dave, why don't you sign your name to one o' these cards an' give it to 'em? That way, if they have any sorta problem, they'll know who t' call."

About half an hour later, SH and I were standing just outside the showroom when they drove up in their 1979 Hondamatic. Frank was driving and he rolled down the window and said, "Chanch chouch."

SH slammed his hand on the roof and nearly shouted, "Well doggone, thank you too. You keep in touch, now, ya' hear?"

They drove off and the car stalled once before they turned east onto El Cajon Boulevard.

As we watched them disappear down Auto Row in El Cajon, I asked, "So what exactly does SH stand for?"

SH turned back into the showroom while joyfully blasting for all within earshot to hear, "It stands for Shut The Fuck Up."

"Ab-so-lutely," agreed Mr. Stan-lee.

Don't Ever Fuck With Me, Asshole

The guys on the lot teased me about many things. I understood that went with being the new guy. But in addition to that, they were convinced they had an abundance of material from which to work. Initially, being from San Francisco was the main source of ridicule. There was no way I could argue their ignorance without losing my job. I have to admit; I almost lost it a few times. But I needed the work, I was outnumbered, and I figured there had to be a clever way to respond. Since they hadn't met Cynthia, I also knew they were cultivating doubts about my having a girlfriend. The fact that I never hung out with them after work, getting drunk and trading fuck stories, was starting to become conspicuously suspicious. Of course, I didn't want them to know much about Cynthia. If they ever found out about PRENARIUS, well, I might as well just go home.

I mentioned their teasing to Cynthia and bless her heart, she took charge of the situation. On a sunny Wednesday in late March, just after noon, she surprised me by showing up with a homemade lunch. That was certainly enough, because she got to meet everyone and they all got to give her the once over.

Of course, because of what she was wearing, the boys didn't stop with the once over. In fact, it was initially difficult to get rid of them. The thing is, Cynthia has always been seriously sexy when she's of a mind and that day, she apparently woke up hungry. She wore a white cotton dress that clung to her like peach fuzz and she made every fiber work to achieve, at best, moderate success in keeping her significantly voluptuous figure contained.

Mr. Stan-Lee had to keep his newspaper on his lap and could not stand up when she sauntered and bounced onto the showroom floor. The rest of the boys were on her like rubber to road, but SH knew the score and generously offered me his office for the lunch hour. I graciously accepted his hospitality, and Cynthia and I did not mind in the least while the entire crew huddled in the narrow hallway and listened as silently as possible while we had what turned out to be our last love making.

When we were finished, even though my lunch hour had come and gone and come again, we moved to a couch in the showroom, ate our food at a leisurely pace and no one cared. We talked about the weather and good Mexican food. Then Cynthia scorched those men to the ground when the subject of sports came up. She reminded the boys that while they may not think much of San Francisco, at least the 49ers had won a Super Bowl. That was more than any of them could say for the Chargers.

She left soon thereafter and SH watched her disappear from sight before proclaiming, "Damn boy, damn."

He then asked, "How come you never told us what you got waitin' for you at home?"

I wanted to laugh, so I bent over and retied my shoelaces while answering, "Boys, if I'd have told you, would you have believed me?"

SH answered, "No, sir. This is one of those seein' is believin' kinda deals. But I'll tell you what. I'll believe you now."

Mr. Stan-lee added, "And she knows her football, too."

SH asked accusingly, "Yeah, boy, how come you never brought that up before?"

I couldn't resist answering, "Gentlemen, football's a weekend thing. To me, unless I'm workin', weekends are for fuckin'. That's the only weekend sport I care about. I don't pay much attention to anything else."

SH shook his head and said, "Damn, boy, I feel like I owe you an apology."

I said, "To hell with that; how about just throwing me a decent goddamn lead? I could use the dough."

SH stared at me for about half a minute, then glanced and winked at Stan before saying, "I got just the thing for you. Day after tomorrow. Got a customer that wants a brand new Civic in blue with all the works. But it'll be another two weeks before our new shipment comes in and he doesn't want to wait that long. I found one at a dealership up in Hawthorne. For a little cut to those boys on the action, we can drive up there, pick it up, drive it back, and close the deal. I'll let you go alone, if you think you can handle it. Jorge from the garage will drive you up there and you can drive the Civic back. Then we'll call the customer and you can do the whole shebang. How about that? You ready?"

"Did I just fuck my woman on your desk?"

"Without a doubt."

"That's right."

So two days later, a mechanic from the garage named Jorge who spoke little English drove me to a dealership in Hawthorne. We did not talk the entire trip, just listened to a Spanish station on the radio and I couldn't help but notice that Jorge had a shit-eating sort of smile almost the entire drive. This became more pronounced as we neared the dealership and he dropped me off. He said, "Buena suerta, mi amigo. Vaya con Dios." His smile was broad and mischievous as he drove away.

I walked into the showroom and told the first salesperson I saw, "Hi, I'm Dave from the El Cajon lot. I'm here to pick up the Civic."

He smiled at me warmly and said, "Wait right here. We'll be right back."

I immediately wondered why he said more than one person would be involved, but I did as I was told. I glanced around the showroom. It looked and smelled like ours, though there was definitely more customer traffic. That made sense, of course. Hawthorne is close to Los Angeles and Orange County is also crammed with people. In fact, I suddenly remembered this was Friday and it was slightly after 4:00 in the afternoon, so I hoped I could be on the road soon. The 405, or San Diego Freeway, was the way home and I knew there was going to be traffic. If it got much later, there was going to be a lot of traffic and my goal was to be back at my lot by 6:00.

Within five minutes, I noticed many salesmen milling about the showroom floor, glancing and smiling at me. I walked to a nearby vending machine and got myself a cola for the road while I nodded acknowledgment to them and wondered why none of them came over to say hello. I also wondered why so many salesmen were suddenly inside. There were obvious customers on the loose outside and that was something that would never, ever happen at our lot. I made a mental note to tell SH how poorly trained the salesmen were at the Hawthorne store. These guys wouldn't last a weekend in El Cajon.

"You must be Dave," came a voice behind me.

I turned around to find a man that looked almost exactly like SH, only a little older, with his right hand extended for shaking, his left hand holding two keys to the car, and his entire being wreaking of hair gel. I was momentarily taken aback by the resemblance, but I shook his hand and said, "Yes, sir, how do you do? Pardon me for saying so, but . . ."

"Yeah, I know, SH is my younger brother. I'm BJ."

Well, of course he was, and I had no doubt he'd earned his initials. Another day, and I might have inquired about them, but I was in a hurry.

I nodded and said, "A pleasure to meet you, BJ. Is there anything I need to know before I roll?"

It seemed the other salesmen were moving closer and again, I wondered why.

BJ said, "Not much, really. She's tight as a virgin. Go easy on her and break her in slow. Keep a light foot and try to go smooth on the shifts."

"Will do," I replied without having any clue what he meant. I asked, "Where's the car?"

"Right behind you," BJ pointed to a car in the center of the showroom.

"Excellent," I said, "just show me the way out."

"Right over there." BJ was pointing to a fairly narrow path between two cars that led to large, open glass doors and a ramp down to the lot with a clear path to the street.

"Great, is there anything else, or anything you want me to tell your brother?"

There was some low conversation among the salesmen I could not understand, but BJ smiled broadly and said, "As a matter of fact, you can tell my brother, that here and now, in front of all these witnesses, before you get into the car, I'm doublin' the pot for you clippin' somthin' on the way out and triplin' it for you gettin' in an accident on the way home."

"I'm sorry, what are you talking about?" I was confused and starting to get a little pissed, as members of BJ's crew began laughing out loud. It was obvious I had been set up for something, but I had no clue what it could be.

"Boy," BJ drawled it out, relishing the moment. "My brother tells me you're an educated young man, a college graduate, with a possible future in our industry. But he also says you can't drive a stick, and the fact is, if you can't drive a stick, you got no bidness sellin' cars. So you just get on behind that wheel, slide this brand new automobile into first gear, and take it home. That's all you gotta do."

Oh shit.

I looked around the room and they were all smiling at me like they'd just made some easy money.

I admitted, "I've never driven a stick shift before."

The laughter grew, but above it bellowed BJ, "We know that boy, and I give you high marks for honesty. If you want, you're welcome to go in my office, call my brother, and have someone drive up here to pick you up. Maybe that girlfriend of yours I heard about can come gitcha."

It's hard to describe how I felt. I didn't think I'd reached the bottom just yet, but I was definitely in free fall. I was also angry. If I hadn't been so outnumbered, I would have enjoyed knocking out as many of BJ's teeth as possible. If I hadn't been so embarrassed, my brief career in the automobile industry would have ended then and there. But I wasn't going to go down that easy.

Instead I attempted to clarify the situation. "So let me get this straight; you and your crew here at the Hawthorne Honda dealership placed a wager with your brother and my crew at the El Cajon Honda dealership. The bet is that you say I can't drive this car back without an accident and my boss, who happens to be your brother, SH, says I can. Did I get that right?"

They were all laughing, but BJ managed to sputter, "That's right."

I continued, "I'm gonna take this brand new Civic, by myself and without any supervision, on the San Diego Freeway near rush hour on a Friday and learn how to drive a stick."

They were laughing real hard and BJ bellowed, "There's just no foolin' you, boy."

I understood the concept of driving a stick. I understood the clutch and theoretically how it worked. What no one knew was that I had practiced shifting in various cars on the lot without actually driving them. Of course, there's a big difference between theory and reality. But given the situation, how I was being fucked with, the nature of the joke and the potential danger, it all came down to one thing . . . balls.

Of course, I might have felt differently except for my own surprise for them.

Remember the little tape recorder that Raves gave me when I wanted to record my neck surgery? The cassette recorder with the built-in condenser microphone and the 120-minute tape? The very same tape recorder that I'd never given back, and had only used once, to record my final group project in Speech 551? I still had it. The exact same small, pocket-sized cassette recorder that I'd placed fresh batteries inside that very morning, along with a brand new 90-minute cassette.

Yes, friends, I smelled shit from the get-go on this thing, so I thought I'd bring along a little backup, just in case. Before I went inside the showroom, I activated that little recorder and made sure the condenser microphone was poking barely enough above my outside jacket pocket.

I stepped pretty close to BJ and said, "I just want to make sure I'm clear on this. I, Dave Morehead, have never driven a five-speed stick shift in my life and you, BJ, understand that."

"That's what my brother told me."

"And you, BJ, are the manager of this Honda dealership."

"Yep."

"Your brother, SH, the manager of the El Cajon Honda dealership, knows this as well and you two decided it would be a fun joke to let me, Dave Morehead, drive this brand new Honda Civic in rush hour traffic without any experience, back to the Honda dealership in El Cajon. Furthermore, if I don't do this, my job might be in jeopardy. Does that pretty much sum it up?"

BJ narrowed his eyes and looked at me curiously, but answered, "Well, that's a pretty wordy way of putting it, but yeah, that sums it up. Jesus Christ, you are a fucking college boy, aren't ya'?"

The only decision that remained for me was whether I had the guts to pull it off. Well, what the fuck? Did I think I could make the drive? Yes, I did. Did I think I would get in an accident? Possibly, but not likely. Would I fuck the car for life by learning to drive a stick on a brand new car? I had no clue, but that really wasn't my problem. That would be between the buyer, the warranty, and the service department. Would I still be selling cars by the time the horribly broken-in Civic started performing poorly? No fucking way. And if I got in an accident, or blew out the clutch, or in any way did anything that got me fired, it would be their word against mine, and quite possibly their attorney against my attorney, along with a little help from my tape recorder.

I smiled, took the keys from BJ, and got in the car. The crew was whooping it up and while my head was buzzing loud, I remember hearing "Holy shit, he's gonna do it" and "Get the fuck outta the way."

I kept smiling, put the car in neutral, and started it. I knew all I had to do was get it rolling and then I could keep it in neutral and let it glide almost to the street. Before I attempted this, I removed the cassette player from my pocket, rewound it a bit, and gave it a quick listen.

Damn, I love Raves. He's right about those condenser microphones. They do the job. BJ sounded crystal clear. I rewound it just a little more and then rolled down my window.

They were laughing so hard, grabbing each other and absolutely ready to tell this story over and over to all their friends and loved ones in Hawthorne. I was smiling broadly back at them and that's when it might have started dawning on a few of them that they had been had.

BJ saw the cassette recorder and stopped smiling. He knew for a fact that he'd been had.

But none of them knew just how badly they'd been had until I hit play, and the last several minutes of conversation between BJ and me played loud and proud through the Honda showroom. BJ's face sagged while the tape played out. As soon as it finished, I made it look like I hit the stop button, but I actually hit the record button again.

The car idled happily in neutral while I said, "I think you'll find this to be a lot less painful than you thought or that you, your crew, and your brother deserve. See, I'm a reasonable man. You just call your brother and you tell him I'm on the way. Then you tell him that I'm going to make the full commission on this sale, along with 25 percent of the wager amount that you and your crew are going to pay. Also, I have to be there when the money arrives just to make sure I get my proper amount for all my pain and suffering."

BJ muttered, "I'd like to give you some pain and suffering."

"I'm sorry. Did I say 25 percent? I meant 50 percent. Anything else you want to add?"

BJ asked, "And what if my brother and I don't agree to your terms?"

I answered, "Well then, you boys get your attorney and I'll get my attorney and we'll sit down with the District Attorney, either San Diego or Los Angeles, or Orange County, or all three, it doesn't matter to me. Then we'll let them work it out. By the way, you got any advice for the drive, seeing how this is the first time I've ever driven a five-speed and I'm real nervous?"

"Yeah," BJ replied, "I hope you crash and die."

I hit the rewind button and played back his last quote before saying, "Damn, you're a stupid son of a gun, aren't ya? Didn't your younger brother ever give you the advice he gave me when I asked him what his initials stood for?"

BJ nodded and the corners of his mouth turned slightly into a smile. He said, "You're gonna do fine in this bidness, boy. Ease it into first and if you hit traffic, put it in neutral and coast whenever you can."

Then he turned and walked away, while the others in his crew stood frozen.

I did as I was told, got it rolling, and coasted easily out of the showroom floor. I stalled once as I turned onto the road, but got it going thereafter and did not stall again while I was still in sight of the dealership.

I'd love to tell you I handled the drive like a pro, but that would be a lie. The traffic was horrible and I stalled that poor car at least fifty times trying to get it into first. I was a little embarrassed and people were laughing at me, but pretty soon I was laughing with them. After about twenty miles of bumper to bumper, we finally got rolling and even when we slowed down, I could keep it in second until easing off the clutch.

I rolled into the El Cajon lot a little after 7:00. I wasn't sure what to expect, but I absolutely did not anticipate the hero's welcome I received. The boys were beside themselves. Apparently, they hadn't stopped laughing since the phone call SH got from his brother.

I was relieved by the response, but I pulled SH aside and said, "I'm serious about what I want. It was no joke. I meant every word."

He slapped me on the back and howled, "I'd sooner fuck a legless whore than cheat you outta what you got comin'. You have my word on it. Boy, don't you worry 'bout a thing. You earned that money, straight up. I knew you had it in you."

Yes, I suppose I did.

SH made good on his word the following Monday when I closed the deal, and an envelope arrived the same day with the payoff from Hawthorne, along with BJ's compliments and best wishes from him and his entire crew.

I called Cynthia, because I wanted to take her out to celebrate, but she had a meeting at PRENARIUS that she simply couldn't miss. So after work, the boys and I hit a bar down the street and I never paid for a single drink. I was on my way.

Way Past Life

"I have to wear wings?"

"Yeah, you'll look great," Cynthia responded with the same enthusiasm that initially attracted me, but could not hold me for much longer. She continued preening in front of the bathroom mirror, making small adjustments to the Kelly Green wig that was the final touch in making her resemble a lime.

The thought occurred to me, and not for the first time, *What in the world am I doing here?* But to admit that out loud would have meant publicly announcing how much of a fool I'd been. I could not do that yet.

So I turned and faced the wings. They were each at least three feet long, bright orange, and utterly preposterous. This could not be true. I looked at the clock and attempted to justify approximately two hours and forty-five minutes of my life dressed like this. I was to wear a full spandex black bodysuit, orange boots (*and they had these in size 13?*) with four-inch long wings on the heels, the aforementioned wings attached to a tight orange vest and, of course, an orange headband with its own four-inch wings on the sides.

I tried to rationalize what I was about to do. Two hours and forty-five minutes. That was less time than it took to play any two of my 90-minute cassettes. No problem. I could do it. And think of the experience. Someday, I'd probably be glad I did this. Better off even. If only I didn't have to wear the wings. Still, I had to admit to a certain humorous curiosity. They were wings, after all.

"My turn in the mirror," I announced boldly, facing the reflection.

"God, you look incredible," Cynthia said before lustily proclaiming, "I can't wait to rip that thing off you later."

Not if I beat you to it, I thought while wishing I were posing for *Marvel Comics*.

And on top of it all, as if the wings and everything else weren't enough, there sat Cynthia. She was a living, breathing, smiling Crème de Menthe. She was the woman for whom I'd left San Francisco. What the fuck was I thinking?

Sorry. I didn't exactly mean that. It wasn't fair to Cynthia. It had not always been like it was at that moment. My goodness, Cynthia could drink and laugh and yes, even fuck with the best of them. And as we faced ourselves that afternoon in the bathroom, while she applied makeup that hid very little, she could still drink. Her laugh was what my friends in Los Angeles remembered best about her, and she could observe and analyze as well as anyone I'd ever met. As for sex, well, Cynthia was great when she was of that mind, and supreme fodder for masturbation. Who knows? Maybe she actually would rip my clothes off later.

It was knowledge in all those things that kept me going. But it was knowledge in *only* those things. I didn't have much else. I was selling cars. I was becoming good at it. I was beginning to enjoy it. I was living in El Cajon, California, a place about as far as you could get from San Francisco and still be in California. It was a place where motorcycles, polyester suits, cults, and a new billboard practically every single day pretty much described the spectrum of human existence. Mercifully, it had San Diego just down the road, but it was still a kissing cousin to the San Fernando Valley of thirty years ago and heading rapidly in that direction. It was April of 1983 just before my low tide. I was selling cars, living with Cynthia, and it was Easter Sunday.

And two times a week, I accompanied Cynthia to the PRENARIUS Center (not in costume) for spiritual guidance. Yes, there it sat at the very bottom of it all. For Cynthia, this was the gateway to Higher Learning. For me, it was one of life's more perplexing piles of shit. Sorry, Cyn, I've got to be truthful here. It was a complete, putrid pile of shit. I suppose I could be diplomatic.

I could say, "It's just not for me" or "Well, that meeting was food for thought" or even "I clearly haven't evolved to a point where I'm prepared to accept."

But in truth, the only words I heard that made sense at the PRENARIUS Center were my own, the first night I went there. People were standing in front of the group, giving testimonials as to their past life experiences. *They actually believe this shit*, I thought. I was also a little bit in awe, because almost everyone in that room had been infamous in their previous lives. There were Hitler (sans mustache), Attila, Lizzy Borden, Julius and Ethel Rosenberg, Judas Iscariot, John Wilkes Booth; the list went on and on. This group was some of the crème de la crème of past life assholes. You had to have some serious blood on your hands to be in that room. The only people who'd had a taste of positive past lives were the ones in charge. How nice for them. Eventually, I was compelled to stand up and say, "I don't know about my past lives, but I do know I don't know what I'm doing here." The entire group applauded warmly.

Give me credit; I stuck it out for two months. Two months assuredly longer than anyone else I knew would have stayed there. Though it must be added, I did not stay there for spiritual guidance. I stayed there because of Cynthia. Her own mother had said, "Maybe she'll listen to you." Of course, it was her parents that helped get her into that crap in the first place.

So in a sense, I was on my own spiritual mission. And boy, was I overmatched? The pseudo psycho analytics of Group Discussion or Sex Roles in Communication at San Francisco State University had prepared me in only a few ways for my PRENARIUS experience. I could listen, I could talk, and perhaps in the smallest of ways, I could persuade.

So I read the books, I listened to the lectures and testimonials; I watched the films and videos. I listened, observed, and tried to understand. And I began to drink at every convenient opportunity.

Of course, it's easy to sit here now and trash what Cynthia and the rest of those misguided and brainwashed people were attempting to do. That's not my intention. Nor is this yet another treatment on the utter waste of time I find most forms of religion or dogma. I am learning to respect people who have integrated spiritual growth into their lives without damning those of us who find it a complete crock. I completely respected Cynthia at the time; though the green wig did somewhat damper her credibility. Plus, the orange wings made me think of a Ralph Bakshi movie.

So that's where things stood on Easter Sunday of 1983 when we stepped from our apartment and headed toward the car.

"Wait a minute," Cynthia ordered. "Stand right there. I want to take a picture of you."

Well, why not? I smiled at her, and then I smiled at the fifteen or so people milling around the pool below, enjoying their Easter in somewhat more conventional attire. Sure folks, Easter is as good a time as any for a costume party. Don't mind me; just go right on with what you're doing. They were swimming, sunning, barbequing, listening to rock and roll, and reading the newspaper. Several stopped what they were doing to stare. I almost told them the drinks are on me; just don't ask me any questions, because I'll tell you no lies.

In the car on the way over, Cynthia asked, "Is there something wrong?" The strain in our relationship was obvious in her voice.

"Yes, but don't worry about it."

Cynthia responded with agitation. "Why don't you just drop me off and go home? I know you're going to hate this."

I thinly rebutted, "No, I'll be all right."

On that note, we parked the car and headed into the Center. Everyone was in costume and if there was ever an example in my life of comfort in numbers, this was it. I wasn't even the only one wearing wings and if such a thing as God exists, He or She certainly viewed our gathering as a vivid example of humans as sherbet.

In addition to being Easter Sunday, this day was significant at the PRENARIUS Center because we were going to have a Healing Session, as presided over by none other than the Archangel Princess Veriold, the eighty-plus years young co-founder, head honcho, and baked potato of PRENARIUS, who in a previous life had been Mary of Bethany, the 13th disciple of Christ.

But first, before we could get to that highlight, we were going to have a little ceremony and it was going to be videotaped. Yes, it seemed the day was going to be even more auspicious than I had been led to anticipate. We were there for the Initiation of Star Center #1, a model depicting thirty-three spaceships landing one atop the other in sort of a gigantic intergalactic pyramid. This was supposed to be an exact replica of the spaceships that were going to land on the acreage owned by PRENARIUS in the foothills east of El Cajon.

When this momentous transforming landing happened, and we were assured it would happen soon, it would be none other than the Archangel Princess Veriold, previously known for changing the fate of France as Joan of Arc, who would then be beamed aboard the top spaceship for her mission to the other world leaders, where steps toward a cognitive world peace could commence.

I tell you no lies.

In single file we marched outside, and in addition to the wings and wigs and flowing robes, we carried banners of other worlds. These weren't just any other worlds. These were other worlds no one but PRENARIUNS had ever heard of, because they were all from other dimensions that scientists from the mere earth had not yet discovered. So with all this and righteous attitude, we lined the street. With videotape rolling, we awaited the arrival of the good Archangel, who'd honed her knowledge of the skies as the 19th century astronomer Caroline Lucretia Herschel.

Cars screeched to a stop and those lucky enough to have cameras snapped the photos rapid fire. They took one for themselves, one for their parents, one for insurance, and one for all the relatives back home and elsewhere to show one of their favorite only-in-California moments.

I looked at those people watching us and for a brief, delightful moment, I was inside one of the cars laughing my ass off, reaching for my journal. I mean would you look at *that* guy? He's wearing wings.

Mercifully, the car carrying the Archangel Princess Veriold, who as Queen Isabella funded the voyage to the New World, soon approached amid all the grace, dignity, and carbon exhaust a '67 Cadillac with a large model plastic spaceship on the roof and letters on the side proclaiming "Welcome Space Brothers" could provide.

Ironically, and with the benefit of hindsight, I must admit this moment truly was one of the highlights of my life. It helped that everyone around me was smiling and laughing with such joy. I damn near dropped my spleen, I was laughing so hard.

Back into the Center we marched and gathered around the model for Star Center #1, all sixty or so of us. The Archangel, who at one time was called Matoaka, but eventually came to be known as Pocahontas, cut the ribbon and we, or should I say they, broke into the traditional PRENARIUS song, "Out of the Spiraling Cosmos."

Unfortunately, the Archangel Princess Veriold, who had her way with the Romans as Cleopatra, was not satisfied with the spirit in which the song had been delivered, so we had to sing it again. I mouthed along and when finished, the Archangel, a.k.a. Hypatia of Alexandria, who lost her life for publicly defending science against religion, delivered a few well-chosen words. I heard none of these, due to a rising roar of disbelief in my head. But Cynthia took my hand and prompted me to sit. Like a lamb being led to slaughter, I complied and the Healing Session commenced.

The good Archangel, a stone-cold fox when she was Nefertiti, was not too pleased with our effort and performance to that point, so what ensued was something akin to spiritual shit hitting the fan. She began walking around the room, glaring at us. Then she moved amidst us, calling upon energies from on high, waving her arms in whirling motions to create waves of spiritual turbulence. She wanted to shake everything loose and cast out the negative energy she sensed in the room.

Seeing as how I was the negative energy, I kept my head down. I also did not want to meet that old woman's eyes, or start staring at her mustache. It would have been all over. It was difficult enough already to keep from laughing out loud. This was made exponentially more difficult when I noticed the Archangel, who amazed them all with her visions as Hildegard of Bingen, had chipped polish on several of her toenails.

People began crying, moaning, screaming and a few dropped to the floor and began to convulse.

Cynthia screamed and shook harder and louder than anyone, which was to be expected due to her junior college training in theater. I could not look at her for very long, despite the independent bouncing of her breasts, which I only then realized were without bra. I was momentarily though substantially aroused, but quickly doused with cold water when I noticed the green mascara running down her face.

Then, a few tortured souls to my right, I noticed a man I previously witnessed giving testimonials as to having been both Napoleon and Nostradamus. At that moment, he was hissing and hacking chunks of phlegm from his lungs onto the linoleum floor below his seat. Cynthia told me later he was channeling a serpent of Satan from a previous life.

Despite my love of surreal drama, I quickly forged a path through the carnage to the men's room, where I unsuccessfully rode through the various crests of nausea. I was thankful. Perhaps this was what Healing Sessions were all about. I might have just shelved the onslaught of a 24-hour virus. I took my time. Given what was going on and still audible from down the hall in the main room, I was in no hurry to rejoin the revelatory spiritualists, or the angry Archangel, who, believe it or not, had also previously been Lisa del Giocondo, the actual Mona Lisa. I waited until the moans became sighs and the cries became sniffs before flushing and returning to the main room.

Once seated again, however, I realized the process was not yet complete. Far from it, we still had to pass through the Flame Room. The very image of the words Flame Room brought forth visions of ritualistic sacrifice, bondage, and torture. I was ready for it. Hell, this was better than anything on cable TV.

In fact, the Flame Room turned out to be a rather beautiful space filled with mirrors and lights. It was designed for peaceful self-reflection. Most who passed through it reacted quietly. There were silent tears and a gaze or two toward the ceiling, painted with stars.

It finally became my turn to reach the threshold and whether by coincidence or design, I came face-to-face with myself. There I was, wings, confusion, and all. I thought, *If my friends could see me now*. The tears gave way to sobs and the sobs gave way to heaves and the heaves gave way to anger and the irrefutable desire to leave that place. Burn the fucking wings and burn the bridges if I had to. Was anything worth this? A woman? Bullshit. I needed a drink so bad.

"Are you ready to go?" I asked Cynthia, and my tone left no doubt I was going with or without her, and, in fact, preferably without.

She knew me well, and she loved me more than that. I will always love her for the gentleness in her expression when our eyes met at that moment.

She said, "No, you go on. I'll see you at home later." I wiped a green streak from her right cheek with my left thumb before she added, "I'm sorry."

"Don't be," I immediately replied and for the first time in about half a year, we were at peace with each other.

I was out the door, into the late afternoon, and off with the wings. I sped home and embraced my blue jeans. I got back into Cynthia's car and placed the perpetual bottle of Jack Daniel's under the driver's seat into my lap. I drove into the desert foothills and positioned the car near the edge of a cliff overlooking the El Cajon Valley, facing northwest. Drink seldom tasted so good. The sunset air was warm and a return to Los Angeles was looking better and better.

The Final Blow Out Evening

It was the Saturday of Memorial Day weekend and there was a party that night at the parents' house of an old friend. Most of us were approaching our mid-twenties and we were still doing the same crap. Christ, that sounded so fucking depressing. It felt like such high school bullshit. Someone's parents were away for the weekend, so the opportunity existed to trash the place with a party. Music would be played at top volume and everyone would agree it was amazing, whether they actually felt that way or not. I was told it was going to be the biggest blow out evening ever, but much improved over the old days. The house had better sound (though no Uphonic Vortex), better booze, lots of women, and best of all . . . there would be virtually limitless blow. Cocaine was everywhere and it was a damn shame. People who used to be nice were assholes when they weren't using and complete phonies when they were shoving that crap up their noses. Several had become addicts and as such, liars and thieves. Cocaine is evil. People who use it cannot be trusted.

It was six weeks since I'd left Cynthia; I was living at home, licking my wounds and trying to figure out the quickest way back to San Francisco. I was twenty-four with no prospects and rapidly dwindling finances. It was low tide in my life.

I was walking more. That was a good thing. Summer was almost upon us, so the air quality was worsening by the day, but walking was still a way to clear the head and help manage the angst. Plus, I was no longer used to driving in LA. I didn't want to become used to driving in LA. I didn't want to acknowledge that I was in LA. I also didn't own a car, so any driving I did was courtesy of Mom or Dad and that was further humiliation.

I had gotten together with a few old friends, but all I did was decompress about where I'd just been and everything I'd gone through. Frankly, I'm not certain any of them believed me, and most didn't give a shit about my tale of woe. Everyone had a tale of woe. They might have been more receptive to mine if I'd so much as listened to theirs. But I didn't. So I'd taken my lumps. It was payback time for me with some of the old gang. They'd heard me trash LA, or heard about me trashing LA for years and years and they were almost gleeful in pointing out the irony of my living in LA and at home. I let everyone have his or her laughs. I faced anyone and everyone that wanted to take a shot. Most took theirs behind my back. The people who confronted me directly were the only ones I hoped would remain my friends. Fuck the rest. And I still couldn't stand LA.

So there was a party that night at a house up a canyon close by and within easy walking distance from the beach. I'd been there before. I would know many people; some of whom I hadn't seen since high school, and most of them would know why I was back in town. It was pathetic. I could almost see LOSER stamped on the forehead of Morehead. The people I didn't know who'd be there either wouldn't give a shit to meet me, or had already heard about me and passed judgment. I was only going because Raves called me the day before and made me promise to come. He told me he had something that was going to blow me away. I told him as long as it wasn't coke.

So I showered and dressed while waxing slightly nostalgic, listening to Elton John sing "Rocket Man" on KNX FM. *Indeed*, I thought, *it's going to be a long, long time.*

I sat down for dinner with Mom and Dad. While mindlessly chewing my third bite of meatloaf, Mom asked what my plans were. I swallowed and told her I was walking to a party but wasn't sure if I'd be home tonight or tomorrow. She said she didn't mean today, she meant my future, my life. I was in no mood for one of those talks. But I was thankful and grateful they had taken me back in, albeit twenty-four and nearly broke. I was also embarrassed for the same reasons. I told them whatever my plans were going to be, they involved getting back to San Francisco as soon as possible.

They both looked a little relieved and I thought, *My god, they want me out of here as much as I want, maybe more.* They didn't say anything else, but glanced at each other and I detected smiles.

I didn't really know what to think or feel, but I completely lost my appetite.

Dad asked if I wanted to borrow his car for the night and Mom immediately said that wasn't a very good idea. Ironically, I agreed with Mom, because at that moment I sensed my sobriety since returning home was going to end dramatically at the party. But I still couldn't help feeling this was further rejection on her part. I felt like I had during the last six months or so prior to leaving home the first time. I got up and Mom asked, with a rather hopeful tone in her voice, if I was leaving soon.

"Yeah, Mom. Really soon. I'll be gone really soon. I promise."

She looked a little confused, but I think Dad understood, though he offered no words of comfort. I felt tears welling and I left the dining room. I put on my shoes and walked quickly toward the front door. Strangely, Mom and Dad were waiting for me and there was no way to pass them without hugs. It's difficult to explain how much emotion I was feeling, and resisting only made it more challenging. Each of them hugged me hard and while that made me feel a little better, the poignancy of the moment also made me feel worse. They loved me, but they wanted my ass gone. What the fuck was I going to do?

The short answer to that, as it turned out, was to find someplace as close as possible where I could be alone before the party. Of course, unless you had a car, or a bedroom in a home where you were still wanted, which I clearly was not, it was nearly impossible to be alone in Los Angeles.

Idiot, I thought, *go to the beach. Get some negative ions into your system and work it out.* Besides, it was sort of the long way to the party. So down the bluff to the beach I quickly walked. Less than an hour of sun remained in the day, and while there were still abundant people, a fully dressed man walking the shore would almost certainly be left alone.

I'll never know if that would have been true, however, because I didn't keep walking. After passing the most congested section of beach, I located a spot about fifty yards from the nearest person where I hoped to simply sit and think. Almost immediately after sitting, however, I started crying. It was a torrent of tears and a convulsion of sobs. I hadn't cried like that since the night before I first left home. I was going to go out with friends that night, but when I was about to leave, I saw Mom sitting in her knitting chair. She didn't look up when I said good-bye and I knew she was in pain. There she was, the woman that had given birth to me and put up with all my bullshit, as I had hers, and her heart was breaking. I suddenly knew she would spend most of the rest of her life in that chair, wondering how I was doing, when I would next come home for a visit, knitting sweaters and booties, mufflers and holiday stockings, baby clothes and woolen caps. I staggered to her, put my head in her lap and we sobbed for almost an hour.

I realized that in all the years since I'd left home that first time, I hardly thought about my parents. Was that the same for everyone? Was that the natural order of things? Out of sight, out of mind? Or was I simply a selfish shit? Were other only children like me? I didn't know, because I hadn't bothered to notice. I felt so guilty about my parents and the shame I'd caused them. I wasn't the only one embarrassed by me. They had to explain to their friends why their only child was living at home again, with no future, or even a plan to speak of. That caused a new wave of pain, and only after remembering that at least they had each other, did I start to release the guilt. Yes, they had each other. What did I have?

That's how I felt at the beach. It wasn't self pity, though. It was loss and longing, regret and remorse, the passing of precious time I would never know again and all the hardship of growing up. It was overdue.

I'm not sure how long I sat there and shook, but at a certain point, I began to feel a weight lifting and something taking its place that was strangely hopeful. I had no idea what it might be, but before I could consider things any further, I noticed someone approaching me from the shore. My eyes were still blurry, but the shape looked feminine. In fact, the shape was quite incredibly feminine.

As I wiped my eyes before attempting to focus, a woman's voice said, "It **is** you."

Oh fucking great, I thought. It was Amanda.

"I heard you were back," she stated with a hint of glee in her voice.

"Uh-huh," I said while trying to focus on the sand.

"And you're staying with your parents, right?"

I nodded.

"Broke, too?"

I kept nodding.

"You're balding, aren't you?"

No reason to stop nodding.

"I've seen you cry on this beach before."

Status quo.

"Aren't you going to look at me and say anything?"

I finally looked, but I said nothing. Amanda was beautiful, even more than before. The hair was back and so was the figure. She was a stunning woman.

We stared at each other and I could see this was a long wished for moment of revenge. Good for her.

Finally, she said, "I've thought about what I would say to you for a long time."

I sighed and then asked, "Is it everything you hoped for?"

"Not quite," she said sounding a little confused. "Not yet."

I asked, "How long has it been?"

"Over three and a half years."

"Well, now's your chance."

She suddenly looked angry. She said, "I always wondered, if I saw you again, would you be the nice person I loved, or the asshole I've hated?"

I looked toward the ocean and considered the question. Finally, I smiled a little and asked, "Amanda, what do you want from me, from this long wished for moment?"

"A truthful answer."

I nodded again and thought, *Okay*. I looked at her and said, "The truth is, I'm glad you grew your hair back, and lost all that weight. You looked horrible the last time I saw you. The truth is, neither one of us were what the other remembered or loved."

She winced slightly and said, "So you're still the asshole."

I shook my head. "No. I don't think so. I don't know, Amanda. I don't exactly know what I am anymore, but I might be closer to finding out than I've ever been. I am truly sorry for that horrible weekend, but I'm glad to be here with you right now. I'm relieved we're finally talking about it. You've become a beautiful woman and you were my first love. That's the truth."

I paused and looked at the sea. The Sea. Yes, it called to me, revealing all truth. And the truth, at that moment, was forgiveness. I smiled and felt renewed. I took a deep breath and then looked at Amanda.

She was also smiling, but beginning to blush as she acknowledged, "I really was a toad, wasn't I?"

"As much as I was an asshole."

This time, it was Amanda who nodded.

I got up.

"Where are you going?"

"Home."

"I remember when you couldn't stand to be there."

"I don't mean my parents' place. I mean San Francisco."

"Right now?"

"Well, no. Not this exact minute. But as soon as I can."

Amanda got up as well. She asked, "Are you going to that party?"

"Regrettably, yes. How about you?"

She smiled with the sort of mischief I remembered from those wonderful days we spent together at the end of high school. I recognized the woman I once loved.

She said, "You couldn't drag me there. There'll be too much coke and too many men still behaving like boys."

I giggled slightly and said, "I know. I don't really want to go, but Raves made me promise."

She said, "Then you probably should go. Raves is a good friend to you. He always has been. He's one of the few."

"You're right." I asked, "Are we going to be friends again?"

She looked at me tenderly. "I don't know."

I felt the delicious onset of bittersweet.

I said, "That makes me a little sad."

"Me too. But it's better than the last time I saw you."

I nodded and smiled.

We hugged, the sun was setting, and I think we both felt free to live our lives. It was a healing moment, at least for me. Before it could get complicated or ruined, I had the good sense to back away and say, "So long Amanda, you look great. I hope you think better of me from now on, and always with more hair."

I heard her giggle as I turned and walked away.

I crossed the Coast highway and veered from West Channel Road onto Chautauqua Blvd. My pace was deliberate, though my step had become considerably lighter. A purpose for the day and perhaps my life was at last showing a glimmer of possibility. I could hear music from at least 200 yards. The song was "Mirror in the Bathroom" by The English Beat. *Perfect*, I thought. *No telling how much cocaine is being consumed to that song.* Voices were only audible at a holler. I was going to a blow out evening. Excellent. I was suddenly so ready.

I walked inside and the auditory assault was intimidating. "Lose This Skin" had begun and I smiled because it was my favorite song by The Clash. That's when I saw Raves and he was currently manning the turntable, so I knew I had been set up. He was nodding his head, and without saying a word gave Rod a signal to take over for him, while directing me with his other hand toward the hallway. I nodded toward Rod, who raised his glass of single malt in my direction.

Raves and I hugged, but he had an agenda and was not going to be taken off task.

He bluntly shouted, "Come with me. There's something I've got to show you."

Of course he did. I was game because Raves had always been the man with the specs.

But even so, nothing could prepare me to be led through the kitchen, past several perfunctory greetings, down the hall, out the back door, to the patio bathed in twilight, and it was there that I saw Gwen.

I looked at Raves, who nodded and said, "Told you." He turned and went inside.

I was elated, but I was so confused. Gwen was luminous. She was wearing a black beret and her red hair fell long and luxuriously over a tight tee shirt that said **I ♠ My Cat.** She was braless and her nipples, so long a fantasy for me, were behaving exactly like mine in the cooling coastal air. Despite this, or perhaps because of it, my mouth opened, my jaw dropped, and I stood stiff as a statue until Gwen walked confidently toward me and took me in her arms.

"Hi David."

"What are you doing here?"

"Waiting for you."

"When did you get here?"

"Last night."

"Why?"

"I've been thinking about you a lot lately. Actually it's been longer than that. But I've been thinking about doing this since you left Cynthia."

"What are you doing?"

"Coming to get you."

"Where are we going?"

"Poor baby, you're really confused, aren't you?"

"How did you know to find me here?"

"It was a well coordinated plan between me, a couple of your friends, and your parents. I got in touch with your old roommate. He put me in touch with Raves. Raves gave me your parents' phone number. They're really worried about you, you know? I mean all of them, your friends and your parents."

"You've talked with my parents?"

"Babe, I met them a little while ago. They wanted me to tell you that was why they wanted you out of the house, not because they're trying to get rid of you. But Dave, I think they are hoping you move out. Watching you mope around is not how they want to spend their retirement years."

My mind was reeling. I was slightly aware of "Crosseyed and Painless" by Talking Heads blasting from the house. Then I asked, "How did you get my tee shirt? I thought I lost it."

Gwen smiled and said, "I stole it from you before I moved to Portland. I wanted something with me that reminded me of you, something that smelled like you. It's still my favorite sleep shirt. But this one isn't yours. I had this one made to fit me. Do you like the way it fits me?"

I nodded and then admitted, "I stole your flowery shirt, by the way."

Gwen nodded, smiled broadly, and said, "I always suspected as much. That's another reason why I stole your shirt."

She gently grabbed my left hand and said, "So Dave, this party looks like it's going to be fun, but would you rather stay here, or leave?"

"Where would we go?"

"Home."

"Home?"

She nodded and said, "I've got a full tank of gas. I've got two suitcases of your clothes, courtesy of your mom, and she'll send the rest. I've got $600 from your dad to cover your initial moving-in costs. I've got a two-bedroom apartment in Noe Valley. You can have your own room, if you want. We can take it slow and be friends for as long as we need, or forever, if that's how it works out. But you're coming home with me right now and sometime tonight, after we've eaten, and been on the road a few hours, we're going to stop and spend the night in a motel."

She paused, then slipped an arm around my waist and pulled me close before adding, "Because Dave, unless I'm very mistaken, I think I still owe you a grudge fuck."

"Let's go," I said huskily and we turned toward the house.

"Go? Go where? You can't go anywhere. You just got here. I haven't even seen you since you've been back. You can't go."

It was my old friend Stein. He was entirely inebriated and his thoughts were in free flow. I introduced him to Gwen.

"It is a pleasure my dear," Stein offered his hand as he gave Gwen a head to chest appraisal. He continued, "A pleasure indeed. Why haven't I met you before? I love your tee shirt. I love what you're doing with that tee shirt. Dave, isn't that your tee shirt? I recall you wearing that tee shirt, but I do not, for the life of me, remember you looking so attractive in that tee shirt. I'd like that tee shirt. I'd like that tee shirt right now. Would you like to give me that tee shirt?"

Gwen was laughing and clearly charmed. I was somewhat shocked. Stein and I knew each other and had partied together, but we weren't exactly close. Then I realized he wasn't speaking to me at all. He was clearly fixated on Gwen. I couldn't blame him.

Stein continued, "No. Clearly you cannot leave yet. Not until I have procured this tee shirt for myself, and its occupant for purposes yet to be determined. I insist you stay. Besides, introductions are in order."

"Stein, I just introduced you. Her name is Gwen."

"I know her name is Gwen," Stein replied with drunken indignation and waved his hand at me in a shoo fly manner before continuing. "She doesn't need another introduction. Her name is no longer the issue. She and I have other matters to pursue. But before we pursue them, I'd like to introduce you to my sister. Dave, my good man, do you remember my little sister, my cutesy wootsy sissy wissy named Tracy?"

That's when Stein stepped to the side and revealed my future. I removed my arm from around Gwen and reached for the extended hand of Tracy. We touched and there was an audible spark of static electricity.

"Oooh, I like sparks," Stein announced. He reached toward Gwen and touched her arm and it caused another spark.

Gwen said, "Dave?"

I said to Tracy, "Hiya Toots. I've met you before."

Tracy said, "Yeah I know, but I can't remember when."

Gwen repeated, "Dave?"

Stein said, "I would gladly discuss trading you a bottle of the best for that tee shirt."

I said to Tracy, "You were really cute, but not so . . . grown up."

"So were you, but you had more hair."

"It was in your brother's kitchen at the 16th Street house in 1979, I think. I was on a visit home from college. I stopped by there with Raves and Rod."

She was starting to remember and said, "You were staring at a poster and laughing."

I asked, "Do you remember what was on the poster?"

Tracy paused and then said, "Some wrestler."

I nodded.

Stein announced, "It wasn't just **some** wrestler. It was Ox Baker. I still have that poster."

He asked Gwen, "Would you like to see that poster? Would you like to trade your tee shirt for that poster? I'm sure we could work out an arrangement."

Gwen grabbed my arm and turned me toward her. She said, "David?" and looked into my eyes. Then she asked, "Did I just lose you?"

I didn't know what to say. I didn't know what was happening, except I wasn't going anywhere unless it included Tracy.

Finally, I said, "Timing, Gwen."

"Dave, are you sure?"

I shrugged slightly and she smiled at me with all the warmth of a true friend. She leaned forward, kissed me softly, and said, "I'll call you in a few days. I want to know how this turns out. And don't worry, I'll tell your parents you're fine, and not to wait up for you."

Then she turned me toward Tracy and added, "It's nice to meet you, Tracy. I look forward to seeing you again. Take care of this man."

Tracy nodded, they shook hands, and the mantle of me was passed.

Gwen grabbed Stein by the arm and said, "I'd like to see what you mean by a bottle of the best."

Stein led Gwen toward the house while saying, "Come with me, my dear," and they were off.

Tracy and I stared at each other with the beginnings of smiles. "The Dreaming" by Kate Bush was playing and I thought, *Nice song, but not the right song. I want to hear the Penguin Café*

Orchestra. I briefly thought of going inside and demanding their second album be put on, but instead I asked Tracy, "Have you heard of the Penguin Café Orchestra?"

With some excitement, she asked, "There's a café with a penguin orchestra?"

I smiled, shook my head, and asked, "Do you want to walk on the beach or something?"

She nodded and followed me to the back gate. When we were almost there, I heard "Beyond Belief" by Elvis Costello beginning and I thought, *Now that's more like it*. That was the last song I heard from my final blow out evening.

We proceeded down the alley and onto Chautauqua, where we turned west for the beach.

Tracy said, "I came with someone tonight."

I could tell she meant a guy, maybe even a boyfriend, though I thought I detected a measure of regret. I looked at her while we walked and waited until she looked at me before responding, "You're leaving with someone else."

Reminders

It's 1986, and two years since Tracy and I moved from LA to San Francisco. We've been married a little over a year, but we were living together within three weeks of meeting. We are albatross, mated for life.

We were going through boxes of old things when we found the journals and notebooks I kept in college and for a little while after. I was embarrassed at first, but it was fun when we invited Gwen over and made a night of it. She lives almost three blocks away in Noe Valley with her partner, Mira. They've also been taking turns with me in the kitchen as we collectively try to find something other than Saltines for Tracy to keep down during her first trimester.

We're thinking about leaving San Francisco, and this time I don't think we'll be back, except to visit. We love it here, but we don't want to raise a family in the city. It's too crowded. Both of us are yearning for more quiet and space, like our camping trips. We're thinking about Oregon, but we're also thinking about Canada. Neither of us likes the direction this country is heading. We're enduring two terms of Reagan and my hunch is we'll get stuck for at least another term with Bush. I don't know how much worse it can get, but I don't think our country has bottomed out just yet. On the other hand, we might not move far away, either. We love this city so much. It's like the last bastion of hope in a world going completely mad with greed and mediocrity. The eighties suck. It's a decade of the worst music, the worst shoes, the worst clothes, the worst hair, and thank goodness mine is leaving me quickly before I succumb, and allow some stylist with a sense of humor to turn what little remains into some last vestige mullet. I don't know. We'll see. I'm cynical about the world, but I'm completely in love with Tracy and that pretty much makes everything okay. Also, we have a lot of friends here, a lot of aunties and uncles who can't wait to see what the Tracy and Dave gene pool produces. I'm kind of curious about that as well.

Two days ago, with fog pouring into the valley, I was dispatched down to the Bell Market on 24th Street for a load of picnic supplies and food. These were for us to consume during the opening ceremonies of the 2nd Gay Games at Kezar Stadium. We have several friends participating, including Tim Yu. As I unloaded the last bags into the Camry, I was ecstatic at the haul. I wasn't certain if Tracy would eat anything I bought, but Gwen, Mira, and I were going to be in jerky heaven, along with good cheese, sourdough, fruit, and other delicious fare. I was walking around to the driver's side when I saw someone who looked familiar walk past the parking lot. I could have let him go, but I'm so happy and in love these days, if that was someone I knew, I wanted to say hello. I want the entire world to know how happy I am. And the person I saw reminded me of someone I had not seen in several years and would love to see again.

I hurried toward the street and turned right, toward Twin Peaks and the cascading fog pouring over the hill. About ten paces in front of me, walking slowly, was the man I thought I recognized. I moved quickly, and caught him after he'd only made three more strides. I walked toward the edge of the sidewalk, because when I passed him and looked, I didn't want to be in front of him, in case I didn't know him.

But I did know him and I was shocked at what I saw.

"Roger?" I asked tentatively.

He stopped and looked at me. He didn't recognize me. Then he did, and barely smiled while saying, "Hello David."

For a moment, I froze, but luckily not long enough for my dismay to take hold and show. I moved toward him and gathered his gaunt and weakened frame into my arms as gently as I intend to hold our children.

"Roger, it's so good to see you," I said as I choked back the emotion.

"You too, sweetie," Roger whispered. "I just wish you didn't see me like this."

We held each other for at least a minute as I simultaneously tried to send him every bit of love in my heart while thinking of what to say next. The truth is always best between friends, so I withdrew slightly and asked, "Roger . . . is it AIDS?"

Before I could finish, he was nodding.

We embraced again.

"I'm sorry."

Roger whispered facetiously, "Well you should be."

This broke the sadness, and our embrace ended.

"I've got my car, can I give you a ride someplace?"

"No, I need to walk. It's good for me. Let's go up to Dolores. There's a park there. We can sit awhile and talk."

Within a few strides, I understood that walking and talking was out of the question. I offered him my arm and he took it gratefully. As we walked, I noticed the faces of people we passed. Many avoided making eye contact with us, just like most do when confronted by the sick, injured, or dying. I realized that under different circumstances, I was just like them. I'd been one of them most of my life. A few looked at Roger and they gave me warm glances of appreciation. A deliveryman with a dolly full of crates impatiently waited for us to pass. He looked at us, then turned his head and shook it in disgust. I glared at him and felt the anger surging toward the surface. I was about to say something rude at the very least, when Roger felt my arm tense and said, "Oooh baby, I'm making you so hard."

I laughed out loud. I burst into laughter so deep that we walked right past the man and all his ignorance.

I asked, "No revenge by fags?"

Roger smiled. "Not today."

"Thanks Roger."

"Thank you, David. You're my champion."

We took several strides before I added, "I used to be just like him, you know."

"I know, sweetie."

We got to the park, across the street from a somewhat claustrophobic pet store where the babble and screeching of birds could be heard from the bench where we sat down. To our left stood the geodesic dome play structure that was often filled with laughing and screaming children, provoking the nearby caged birds to even greater cacophony. At that moment, however, it was empty. Overcast was threatening to take over, but the sun was still alternately breaking through and then hiding behind the fog. It was beautiful. It was a summer day in San Francisco. We sat in silence for several minutes while we took it all in and Roger caught his breath.

He finally asked, "Where's Cynthia? Is she still in that nutty cult?"

"No," I was happy to tell him. "She's married, completely agnostic, and getting her teaching credentials in North Carolina. We're still friends."

"I'm glad."

I dreaded his next response, but asked, "What about Little Tim?"

He told me, "Tim is gone, along with almost everyone else you met, I think, except Hilary. He's either the luckiest slut I've ever known, or he has the immune system of a duck."

I couldn't help but giggle.

That made Roger happy and he asked, "Where have you been? What are you doing? What's this on your finger?" He touched my wedding ring.

I smiled and told him everything I could about Tracy. I watched his face brighten from the light of true love. He was thrilled when I told him we're expecting.

"Do you know what it's going to be?"

I nodded.

"Well?"

I leaned over and whispered into his ear.

He said, "You must be so happy."

I smiled and Roger put his head on my shoulder. We sat in silence. He closed his eyes and I watched the ballet of light and shadow.

Finally, I asked, "Roger, what about you? You disappeared right after I moved away. Were you already sick then?"

"Yes."

My heart was breaking, but I continued, "I tried to find you when I moved back, and my old roommate tried to find you years ago. When he didn't . . ." and my voice cracked.

"Oh baby," Roger said and sat up. "Don't worry about me. I'm still here. You just caught me on a lousy day. At least, it was lousy until I saw you."

I bit my lower lip and stared down 24th Street.

Roger said, "You're going to be a weepy Daddy, aren't you?"

I nodded.

"That's good. We need more of those."

I composed myself, but before I could ask him questions about his condition, Roger placed his right hand over my left and asked, "David, how's your drinking?"

I was stunned. It was a question no one had ever asked me. Roger had never seen me drunk. The look of shock on my face seemed to delight him.

He said, "Over the years we've been out of touch, I always regretted not asking you, or talking with you about this."

I said, "Roger, I might be wrong, but I don't think you've ever seen me have even one drink."

He nodded. "That's true, and that's why I know you have a problem. You were so adamant about not drinking at times, and then I noticed you had alcohol in your home. You never offered me a drink, not even a beer. I knew your roommate didn't drink, but when I'd come over on consecutive days, there was always less beer in the fridge, less vodka in the freezer, or an empty bottle in the trash. A couple times, I left really late, and returned pretty early, so that meant you started drinking after I went home. I wasn't snooping, but it was something I noticed and it was unusual. It seemed like you were trying to hide your drinking from me, like I'd think less of you if I knew you liked to get drunk. Were you?"

I don't think I've ever been busted like that. But instead of shame or guilt, I felt relief, and I smiled, because I had good news to report.

I said, "It's been almost seven months since I had any alcohol. I stopped when we became pregnant. But I haven't been really drunk since Tracy's 21st birthday a couple years ago. Neither has she. We both got alcohol poisoning and neither of us ever want to feel like that again."

Roger said softly but emphatically, "Good."

I admitted, "You're right, of course. I didn't want you to know. It was silly. I didn't have a problem. I just didn't want you to think I did."

Roger insisted, "But you do have a problem."

"Well, I did," I sort of agreed.

Roger gripped my hand and said, "No David, it doesn't work like that. You're always going to have a drinking problem, and the only way you can stop it is by not drinking. Trust me, I've seen this. Promise me you're going to stay sober."

I said, "I promise my drinking is not going to become a problem again."

He scolded, "That's not good enough."

I responded defensively, "That's the best I can do right now. I have to think about this. Give me some time."

Roger nodded, sighing with resignation and said, "Okay. Just as long as you always remember, you have a problem with alcohol."

I reached my right hand over and patted his while saying, "Trust me Roger, I'll remember now. Thanks, Mom."

Roger quickly responded, "Don't you dare patronize me."

"I'm not," I defended, giggling a little. "You caught me. I was bad. I won't be bad anymore. I swear."

"Good," he answered, but then added, "If Tracy was here right now, I'd tell her the same thing. Promise me you'll tell her about this."

"I promise, Roger. Jeez. If you'd like, you can tell her yourself. You want to come over and meet her? We live close by. I've told her so much about you."

"Not today, David. I'm tired. Plus, she's pregnant and I'm . . . not well. I need to get home soon. Let's walk."

Because it was downhill from the park, we moved more quickly than we had earlier, but we still didn't speak until we got to my car. Once again, I asked Roger if I could give him a ride.

He shook his head and said, "No thanks, I'm close."

I wasn't sure what to say. I didn't want him to leave.

Roger leaned forward and kissed my cheek. Then he whispered, "David, let me go."

"Is this good-bye?"

"Of course not, you'll see me again."

"When, where?"

"In Heaven. Remember? You'll see me soon."

He backed up, winked, turned, and almost jauntily walked away.

Someone in a waiting car tapped their horn lightly because they wanted to know if I was leaving. I nodded, but I waited for Roger to disappear from sight before I got in my car and went home.

The next day we dressed in layers, piled into the Camry, and got to Kezar early for the Opening Ceremonies of the 2nd Gay Games. We didn't want to miss a moment of the parade of athletes and we were successful. Before the parade, however, just after we sat down, Connie and Jessica, who were still together and totally committed, joined us. We yelled and waved hello to Dr. Monica Lewin, who smiled warmly and waved back. She was popular in the crowd the entire day.

We made a spectacle of ourselves when we spotted Tim Yu during the parade of athletes. He walked with such confidence and I couldn't believe he was the same shy and uncertain man I'd met years before. When he got to a point on the track nearest where we were seated, our group stood and started chanting, "YUHOO, YUHOO, YUHOO," and we kept at it until he suddenly looked into the stands and saw us. Tim smiled broadly, waved wildly, and then stopped and posed on the track, flexing all his muscles. The crowd loved it. I wasn't there days later when he ran his hurdles event, but I was told that when his name was announced before the start of the race, several in the crowd, and not just people that knew him, chanted "YUHOO, YUHOO, YUHOO." I was also told that Tim ran his all time personal best.

Other than that wonderful moment, the best part of the Opening Ceremonies for me was when I got to see Dr. Tom Waddell for the first time in person and then I heard him speak. We didn't know, at the time, that about four weeks earlier he found out he had AIDS. We didn't know he wouldn't live to see another Gay Games, or that his inspiration would one day become the largest sporting event in the world. All I knew on that glorious day at Kezar was that I was sorry I had never met him, because he reminded me of Roger. I started to cry. Before I could so much as offer a word of explanation, I found myself being held, touched, and comforted by Tracy, Connie, Jessica, Mira, and Gwen. Damn, I was happy to be a man.

Acknowledgments

The author wishes to thank the following people for their help and support in the making of this book: Karen Gordon and Ned Takahashi for editing, Dave Dondero for the cover photo, Art Rogers for the author photo, Lauren Pizzi and Joseph Rende for being my audio book cast, the entire staff of the History department in the Main Branch of the San Francisco Public Library, Tiffany Taira for video work, the Big and the Boo, and finally to Karen Hickey, for her cover design, video edits, and for being the love of my life.

This book is a work of Fiction. Any resemblance between the characters in this book to actual persons, living or dead, is coincidental.

Biography

Started as a muleskinner. Worked my way to camp cook. Married the first woman who didn't look away from me when I smiled at her. Spawned a couple of look alikes. Stopped eating cheese, and lived a happier life. Retired to write fiction, against the advice of everyone.

Other works by Jeffrey Hickey include *The Coach's Son*, *Wages Creek* and *Bats and Bones*. He is currently working on his next novel, *Scary, Man*. Look for all these works in Print, Kindle, and Audio Books.

Follow Jeffrey Hickey

http://www.facebook.com/BignBooatDerZoo

jeffreyhickey.com

Support Independent Authors

Made in the USA
Charleston, SC
10 May 2012